"There was a ti... even know my first name,"

Bethany said quietly.

"I knew," Joshua whispered. He was so close behind her that she could feel his warm breath against the side of her neck. "I've always known."

A shiver of awareness scooted down her spine as he gently cupped her shoulders, drawing her back so her body fit against his. His movements were slow, deliberate, as though he expected her to object, to pull away.

Bethany went completely immobile. She couldn't have moved had her life depended on it.

He lowered his mouth to the slender curve of her neck. The instant his lips touched her skin, heat erupted like a fiery volcano throughout her body.

"There I was, at the most important meeting of my life," he whispered, his voice husky and moist against her flushed skin, "and all I could think about was you."

Dear Reader,

Welcome to Silhouette—experience the magic of the wonderful world where two people fall in love. Meet heroines that will make you cheer for their happiness, and heroes (be they the boy next door or a handsome, mysterious stranger) who will win your heart. Silhouette Romance reflects the magic of love—sweeping you away with books that will make you laugh and cry, heartwarming, poignant stories that will move you time and time again.

In the coming months we're publishing romances by many of your all-time favorites, such as Diana Palmer, Brittany Young, Sondra Stanford and Annette Broadrick. Your response to these authors and our other Silhouette Romance authors has served as a touchstone for us, and we're pleased to bring you more books with Silhouette's distinctive medley of charm, wit and—above all—*romance*.

I hope you enjoy this book and the many stories to come. Experience the magic!

Sincerely,

Tara Hughes
Senior Editor
Silhouette Books

DEBBIE MACOMBER

Almost an Angel

Silhouette *Romance*

Published by Silhouette Books New York

America's Publisher of Contemporary Romance

To Sue Dailey,
the woman who allows me to write guilt-free

SILHOUETTE BOOKS
300 E. 42nd St., New York, N.Y. 10017

ISBN: 0-373-08629-6

First Silhouette Books printing February 1989

Printed in the U.S.A.

Books by Debbie Macomber

DEBBIE MACOMBER

has quickly become one of Silhouette's most prolific authors. As a wife and mother of four, she not only manages to keep her family happy but also aims to keep her publisher and readers happy with each book she writes.

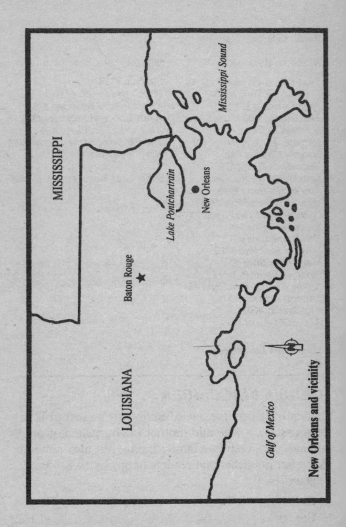

MISSISSIPPI

LOUISIANA

Baton Rouge

Lake Pontchartrain

New Orleans

Mississippi Sound

Gulf of Mexico

New Orleans and vicinity

Chapter One

Bethany Stone's nimble fingers flew over the keys of her IBM typewriter. Tears blurred her soft blue eyes as she typed the few short sentences that would terminate her employment with Norris Pharmaceutical Company and J. D. Norris. This was it, the end, she'd had it up to her ears and beyond!

Any woman who would waste her life for a man who treated her like a robot deserved to be unemployed. Bethany had played the part of a fool for three long years, perfecting the role. But no more! It was long past time for her to hold her head high, walk away and never look back.

The words from a militant protest song played loudly in her mind as Bethany signed her name with a flourish at the bottom of the letter. She straightened. For all the attention Joshua David Norris had paid her, she might as well have been a machine. Oh, he might miss her efficiency the first few days, but he'd soon find a replacement and then she would quickly fade from his memory. A year from now, if someone was to casually mention her name, Bethany was convinced he would have trouble remembering who she was.

The intercom beeped unexpectedly. "Miss Stone, could I see you a moment."

With a determination born of frustration and regret, Bethany jerked the letter of resignation from her typewriter and stood. As an afterthought, she reached for her dictation pad. Her shoulders were stiff and her back ramrod straight as she opened the door that connected the outer office with the executive suite. She exhaled once, hard, and filled her steps with purpose as she marched into the executive office.

Joshua was scribbling notes across a yellow sheet of tablet paper in his thin spidery scrawl. He didn't bother to glance up when she entered the room, and for a few brief moments, Bethany was given the opportunity to study the man she loved—fool that she was. He was sitting, the muscles in his broad shoulders relaxed. Not for the first time, Bethany sensed the complexity of this man's character. He was strong and mature yet headstrong and obstinately blind. Often she'd been a witness to the way he buried his pain in the tight fabric of control that he wrapped around himself. In some ways, Bethany knew Joshua Norris better than he knew himself. And in others, he was a complete stranger.

His hair was dark brown with faint highlights of auburn, the result of many hours spent in the sun, sailing on Lake Pontchartrain. His brows were thick and drawn together now in concentration as he jotted down his thoughts. The smooth contours of his handsome face were broken by a square angular jaw that revealed an overabundance of male arrogance.

His eyes were a deep rich shade of brown that reminded her of bitter coffee. She knew from experience that they could reveal such anger that she was sure one look was capable of blistering paint off a wall. And then there were those rare times when she'd seen his gaze flitter over the photo of his daughter, Angie, which rested on his desk. Bethany had seldom witnessed a look more gentle. All she knew was that Angie lived somewhere in New York and was being raised by his wife's family. In all the years that Bethany had been employed by Joshua, he rarely mentioned his daughter. From everything she knew of the man, which was considerable since they spent so much time together, J. D. Norris didn't seem interested in long-term relationships and created a thick outer shell that often seemed impenetrable.

Joshua dropped the pen on top of the yellow tablet, leaned back in his chair and pinched his thumb and index finger over the bridge of his nose.

"Miss Stone, do we have any aspirin?"

"Yes, of course." His request caught her by surprise. Quickly she crossed the room to the wet bar, returning momentarily with a water glass and two tablets.

He gave her a fleeting smile of appreciation. "Thanks."

Now that she thought about it, Joshua *did* look slightly pale. "You aren't feeling well, Mr. Norris?"

He shook his head, then widened his eyes as though he regretted the action. "I've got a beast of a headache."

"If you'd like, I'll cancel your afternoon appointments."

"That won't be necessary," he informed her crisply. He tore the top sheet off the tablet and handed it to her. "Could you have these notes typed up before you leave tonight?"

"Of course." The letter of resignation remained tightly clenched in Bethany's hand. She hesitated, wondering if she should give it to him now, then quickly decided against it. The last thing Joshua needed was another problem.

His glance revealed his annoyance. "Was there something more, Miss Stone?"

"N-no." She did an abrupt about-face and left the office, her knees trembling.

Ten minutes later her best friend and roommate, Sally Livingston, stuck her head inside the door. "Well, what did he say?"

Bethany pretended to be busy, but she should have known Sally wouldn't be easily thwarted. Her friend advanced toward her desk, folded her arms and tapped her foot, waiting impatiently until Bethany had finished typing her sentence.

"Well?" Sally demanded a second time.

"He didn't say anything."

Her roommate's brow crimped into a tight frown, "Nothing? You handed J. D. Norris your two-week notice and he didn't so much as respond?"

There was nothing left to do but confess, but still Bethany avoided looking in Sally's direction. "If you must know, I didn't give it to him."

"Bethany," Sally whispered angrily. "You promised."

"I—I wrote the letter."

"That at least is a start."

"I was going to give it to him—honest, but he has a headache and he looks absolutely terrible. The timing just wasn't right, and you know how important that is in these situations."

"Beth, this is crazy! The time will *never* be right—you've got to do it today, otherwise you'll end up putting it off for God knows how long."

"I know." Defeat weighted Bethany's voice. She'd promised Sally and herself that she wasn't going to delay this unpleasant task another day, and here she was looking for an excuse to put off the inevitable. "I'll do it Friday then."

"What do you think today is?" Sally asked, sending her dark gaze straight through her.

"Oh," she mumbled, and lowered her eyes. "Monday morning then—first thing—you have my word on it."

Sally unfolded her arms and rolled her eyes. "I've heard that line before."

"All right," Bethany cried. "I'm a weak sniveling mass of Jell-O. I've got all the backbone of a...a worm."

"Less!"

Bethany paused and surveyed her friend through narrowed eyes. "What could be less than that?"

"You!"

"But, Sally," Beth said in self-defense, "Mr. Norris looks terrible. He's really pale and his head hurts and I think he might be coming down with some Asian virus."

"It serves him right."

"Sally!" It wasn't Joshua's fault that Bethany had fallen in love with him. The man didn't so much as guess that Bethany cared a whit about him.

It was Bethany's own fault for allowing her heart to become attached to a man who chose to live his life without emotional commitments. It wasn't that he ignored Bethany in particular. He seemed to be estranged from all women, or at least that was what Bethany had assumed. The divorce from, and later the death of, his ex-wife had left him hard and bitter toward the opposite sex. On the other hand, maybe it wasn't all women Joshua didn't like but just her. The thought was a depressing one. In the end, either way, Bethany would only be hurt. She had to leave him—it was best for everyone involved.

If only Bethany knew how to crack the thick facade Joshua had erected over the years. If she'd had a little more experience or been a bit more sophisticated, then perhaps she could have come up with a surefire plan to win his heart. But as it was, she'd simply stayed on, hoping one day Joshua Norris would look up at her and some mysterious magic would change everything. Twinkling lights would go off in the distance and little hearts would pop up around her head, and after all these years he would recognize the love she'd stored up just waiting for him to discover.

"All right," Bethany returned forcefully, her hands knotting into tight fists of steely determination. "I'll do it."

"Today?" Sally looked skeptical.

"I'll place the letter on his desk when I leave." It was a coward's way out, but when it came to standing up to Joshua Norris, no one was going to award Bethany a medal for valor.

"Good girl." Sally patted her across the back much like a general would before sending a raw recruit into battle. "Meet me at Charley's when you're through here."

Bethany nodded. Charley's was a popular New Orleans cocktail lounge. The two had taken to stopping there and relaxing with a drink on Friday nights. A reward of sorts for making it through another difficult work week.

"I'll see you there," Bethany said, and nodded once. She inhaled a steadying breath, forcing herself to accept her destiny. Once Joshua left the office, she would simply walk inside, place her resignation on his desk and be done with it. Then there wouldn't be any time for second thoughts and looming regrets. She had to forget the man and get on with her life before she woke up a disillusioned and unhappy old maid.

It was after six by the time Bethany made her way into the crowded cocktail lounge. Sally had already found a table, and when Bethany paused to glance around, she saw Sally stand up and give a short wave. Bethany forced a smile to her lips and joined her friend. When the waitress strolled by, she pointed at Sally's drink and said, "Give me whatever she's having, only make it a double."

The woman nodded and turned away.

"You actually did it," Sally murmured, her voice low and incredulous. "You finally handed J. D. Norris your notice."

The mint julep arrived and Bethany drew her wallet from inside her purse to pay for it. "Not yet, but I'm determined that I will."

"Not yet," Sally echoed, her eyes dropping to Bethany's drink in the tall frosty glass with a sprig of mint. "Then why the double?"

"Because I'm a weak, sniveling, spineless—"

Abruptly Sally stopped her, looking disgusted. "We've already determined that."

"Listen," Bethany said thoughtfully. "I've been giving some thought to my problem and I think I may be doing Joshua Norris a disservice."

"How do you mean?"

The hum of conversation and a Dixieland band playing in the distance caused Bethany to raise her voice, but only slightly. She leaned her head closer to her roommate's. "I've never given Joshua a chance." At Sally's perplexed look, she hurried to add, "He hasn't a clue to the way I feel about him . . . I think I should have the courtesy to at least tell him."

"Oh, Beth," Sally muttered, and shook her head several times in a pathetic little twist. "The man has to be blind not to know how you feel. The entire company is aware you love him.''

Bethany paled. She actually felt all the blood rush from her face and pool at her ankles. When she spoke, her voice came out scratchy, high-pitched and weak. "Everyone knows?''

"Maybe not janitorial."

"Oh, God." She took a long sip from her straw and nearly coughed at the potency of her drink. Tears stung her eyes and she shook her head, hoping to lessen the powerful effect.

"All right, I was just joking. Not everyone knows—but enough people do.''

"Sally, don't joke about something this important. All I want is to handle J. D. Norris in my own time and in my own way."

"What do you plan to do?'' Sally asked in a husky whisper. "Saunter into his office, bat your eyelashes a couple of times and suggest children?''

"No...I...I don't know yet." She pushed the short dark curls from her temple. She was twenty-five and behaving like a bungling naive teenager.

"You've had three years to tell him the way you feel. What makes you think you can do it now?''

"I . . . I've never actually *told* him."

"Not outright, true, but honestly, Beth, give the matter some thought here. You're much too gentle-natured and sweet to come right out and tell J. D. Norris you've fallen in love with him. He's bound to give you one of those famous dark looks of his and send you running for cover."

"But I've been thinking..."

"The first time is always hardest," Sally joked. She reached for a handful of salted peanuts, munching on them one at a time.

Bethany's shoulders sagged with defeat as she reached for the salted nuts. "I'm hopeless."

"No," Sally answered, her look sobering. She hesitated and popped another peanut in her mouth. "But J. D. Norris is. If you were going to fall in love, why did it have to be with him?" Her elbows rested on the tabletop, and another peanut found its way between her lips. Sally's eyes narrowed with a thoughtful frown. "Beth, face it, the man's soured on women, soured on marriage, soured on life. He's the big bad wolf and you're an innocent lamb. As your best friend, I refuse to stand by and let you get your throat slit."

"But . . . he's wonderful." Bethany knew Joshua in ways the other employees of Norris Pharmaceutical couldn't. She'd been a silent witness to his generous contributions to charity. She admired his unwavering dedication to medicine. Bethany was sure there were times when others viewed him as harsh, but she'd never known him to be unfair or unkind. In the three years she'd worked for him, there had been enough glimpses of the real man inside to convince her that the exterior of indifference he wore was only a thin shell.

Sally chewed on the peanut as though it were rawhide, then paused, surprise widening her gaze and giving her away. "Don't look now, but . . ."

Instantly Bethany jerked her head around.

"I told you not to look," Sally berated her friend. "He's here."

"Who?"

Immediately Sally's dark eyes narrowed into thin slits, and her right eye started to twitch, a sure sign she was irritated. "I thought you said your precious Mr. Norris was coming down with some dreadful virus."

Bethany's brow knit into a thick frown. "He did have me get him aspirin." But Sally wouldn't recognize how unusual that was.

"Well," Sally said, looking properly disgusted, "he seems to have made a miraculous recovery."

"He's here?" Bethany rose halfway out of her chair before Sally jerked her back down. "But he really *did* look terrible this afternoon." She felt the muscles in her throat tighten with dread. "He's with someone, isn't he? That's the reason you don't want me to look." Already her mind was conjuring up a tall luscious blonde—someone she could never hope to compete against.

"Nope." Sally's eyes followed him. "He just sat down at the bar." The handful of nuts was positioned in front of her mouth. "You know, now that I have a chance to get a good look at him, you're right."

"About what?"

"He is . . . I don't know, compelling looking. He's got a lean hardness to him that naturally attracts women. An inborn arrogance, if you will."

Sally wasn't telling Bethany anything she hadn't already known—for years. "You're sure he's alone?"

"I just told you that."

Bethany clenched her hands together in her lap. "What's he doing now?"

"Ordering a drink. You're right about something else, too. He doesn't look the least bit like himself. Not exactly sick, though."

Bethany couldn't stand it any longer. She twisted her chair around so she could get a decent look at her employer herself. The room was filled with cigarette smoke, resembling an early-morning bayou fog. She braced herself, not sure what to expect. But when her gaze skimmed over Joshua, she stiffened all the more and experienced a rush of concern. "Something's wrong," she whispered, surprised she'd spoken aloud.

"How can you tell?" Sally wanted to know, her voice barely above a whisper as though the two of them were on a top secret reconnaissance mission.

"I just can. Something's troubling him. Look at the way he's leaning over his drink...how his shoulders are slouched. I wonder what happened. Something's got him terribly worried—I can't remember the last time I saw him look so rejected...so distressed."

Sally shook her head. "I don't know where you get that. The only reason he's slouching like that is because he wants to be left alone. Didn't you ever read that book on body language? He's letting others know he isn't in the mood for company."

"Maybe." Thoughtfully Bethany gnawed at the corner of her lower lip. "But I doubt it." Without any real plan in mind, she pushed back her chair, reached for her purse and drink and stood.

"What are you doing?" Sally demanded in a tight whisper.

"I'm going to talk to him."

Sally briefly touched her arm. "Be careful, sweetie, wolves have sharp teeth."

Bethany's returning smile was weak at best. Her heart was pounding like a ramming disk against a concrete wall as she advanced toward Joshua Norris. Luckily the stool beside his was vacant. She perched her five-foot-five frame atop it and set her mint julep on the bar, folding her hands around the cool drink. She gave him a minute to notice her and comment.

He didn't.

"Hello," she said softly.

It seemed like an eternity before he twisted his head around to look at her. When he did, surprise briefly widened his intense dark eyes. "Miss Stone."

Bethany took another deep swallow of her drink, seeking the courage it would give her. But for the life of her, she couldn't think of anything profound to say. She tossed a glance over her shoulder and Sally's eyes rounded as she nodded encouragingly.

"I didn't know you frequented Charley's," Bethany managed at last, amazed at how strange her own voice sounded.

"I don't." His words were clipped, discouraging any further discussion.

"Are you feeling better?"

He turned back to her then. "Not particularly."

The bartender strolled in their direction and Joshua motioned to the tall thin man that he wanted a refill. The man poured Joshua another shot glass of Scotch, then cast Bethany a questioning glance.

She shook her head. She had a one-drink limit, and as it was, the alcohol was already rushing to her brain.

"I have aspirin in my purse if you need some."

"I don't." He answered without looking in her direction, as though he wished she would get up and walk away. He hadn't sought her company and the stiff way in which he sat told her as much.

Not knowing what else to do, Bethany took several more sips from her mint julep. The potency of each one burned a path straight to her stomach. Feeling tipsy and more than a little reckless, she lightly placed her hand on his forearm. "We've worked together all this time, I hope you feel you can trust me."

"I beg your pardon." His hard gaze cut into her.

"Won't you tell me what's wrong?"

"What makes you think anything is troubling me?"

"I've worked for you for three years. I know when something's wrong. I've seen that look in the past and I..."

"I am well aware of the length of your employment, Miss Stone—"

"Bethany," she interrupted, her unflinching gaze meeting his. "I've worked for you all these years, and I think you should know my first name is Bethany."

His eyes formed glacial slits. "And what makes you think that I care to know your first name? Because, rest assured, I don't."

Her breath felt trapped in her lungs, and scalding color erupted in her cheeks. She'd seen Joshua be cold and insensitive before, but never anything like this. The look he gave her was more than embarrassing...it was humiliating. The edge of his mouth turned upward in a half sneer, as though he were viewing something distasteful. His intense gaze cut her to the quick before he dropped it to her fingers, which were lightly pressing against the sleeve of his jacket.

Uncharacteristic tears pooled in Bethany's eyes. Slowly, as though in slow motion, she withdrew her hand from his arm. Her whole body went numb. The uselessness of it all hit her then, more poignantly than all the lectures Sally had given her, more cutting than her own soul-searching efforts. The message in Joshua's taut gaze was sharp, hitting its mark far more effectively than he would ever guess. He didn't know who she was; he didn't care to know. The world he'd created was his own, and he wasn't ever going to invite her or anyone else inside.

Her gaze didn't waver from his as she slid off the bar stool and took one small step in retreat. "I won't bother you again." The words managed to wrestle through the stranglehold that gripped her throat muscles. "I'm sorry... really sorry."

Bethany didn't know where she was going. All she knew was that she had to escape before she humiliated herself further and burst into hopeless tears. She walked past Sally's table without looking at her friend and maneuvered her way through the crowded lounge and outside into the chill of the January night.

For a moment she thought she heard someone call her name, but she wasn't up to explaining what had happened to Sally or anyone else. All that mattered was escaping. Increasing her pace, she ran across the brick-lined street and down the crowded sidewalk on Decatur Street that bordered the popular French Quarter. The roadway was crowded, the walkways busy, but Bethany kept her head down, walking as fast as her feet would carry her. Not knowing where—not caring.

"Miss Stone. Wait."

Bethany sucked in her breath at the sound of Joshua's impatient demand, swung her purse strap over her shoulder and pushed herself to walk faster.

"Bethany."

She heard the sound of his running footsteps and jerked the heels of her hands over her eyes to wipe away any evidence of tears.

Surprisingly, once Joshua caught up with her he didn't say a word. She must have continued walking half a block with him, their steps in unison, before he spoke.

"I owe you an apology."

"I . . . was being presumptuous," she said, offering him an excuse. She'd done it so many times before that it came as second nature. "Simply because we work together doesn't mean you need confide in me."

"Perhaps, but there was little reason to be rude." Once again his words were brusque, but any anger seemed directed inward.

Neither spoke for a minute, and when Bethany looked up, she noted they were walking past Jackson Square. Several park benches were spread across the lush green lawn in front of the statue of Andrew Jackson on horseback.

Joshua motioned toward an empty bench. "Would you care to sit for a minute?"

Bethany offered him a feeble smile and calmly took a seat, although her heart continued to beat erratically. Joshua sat down beside her. After what seemed a hundred years, he spoke. "It's Angie."

At the mention of his young daughter, alarm worked its way through Bethany and adrenaline shot into her bloodstream. She twisted her upper body so she was facing Joshua, her hands gripping his sleeve. "Is she ill? Has she had an accident?"

"No, no." Abruptly he shook his head. "As far as I know, she's in perfect health."

Bethany relaxed, dropped her hands and slumped against the iron railing that made up the back of the park bench.

Joshua sighed, his look bleak, distressed. "What do you know about children, Miss Stone?"

"Very little, actually." She was an aunt several times over, and although she dearly loved her nieces and nephews, they lived in Texas and she only saw them on summer vacations.

"I was afraid of that." Roughly he splayed his fingers through his hair. "Damn it all, I don't know what the hell I'm going to do."

Questions were popping up like fizz from a soda can in Bethany's mind, but after her earlier attempt to draw him out, she dared not drill him for information.

"Angie's mother and I were divorced shortly after she was born."

He paused as though he expected Bethany to make some wide sweeping statement. She had none to offer so kept her half-formed thoughts to herself.

"Over the years, I've visited her when I could," he went on, his brooding gaze seeking hers. "God knows, I've tried to do everything I could moneywise."

"She's a beautiful little girl," Bethany murmured, not knowing what else to say. Angie's photo was updated regularly and each time Bethany looked at it she saw the promise of rare beauty in the ten-year-old.

Joshua nodded sharply, his brow furrowed with a brooding frown. "The thing is, I don't know a damn thing about being a father."

"But you've been one for the past ten years," she couldn't help reminding him.

"Not really," he murmured, his facial features remaining tight. "Not a real father." He stood then and rubbed his hand along the back of his neck. "I've never felt more inept in my life."

Bethany was sure that the sensation was foreign to him. In all the time she'd worked for Joshua, she'd never seen him as upset or unsure.

As though forgetting his own problems for the moment, he hesitated and stared down at Bethany. His hard gaze softened perceptibly and a half smile flittered at the edges of his sensuous mouth. "You didn't deserve the treatment I gave you earlier. I truly *am* sorry."

An earthquake wouldn't have been powerful enough to tear Bethany's gaze from his. In three years, this was the most personal comment he'd ever made to her. Forgetting her earlier reluctance, she asked him softly, "Won't you tell my what's happening with Angie?"

He nodded and slumped down into the seat beside her. "I talked with my mother-in-law yesterday afternoon. It seems both my in-laws have been in poor health recently."

Bethany nodded, encouraging him to continue.

"They feel it's time for Angie to come live with me. I'm supposed to pick her up at the airport in a couple of hours." He paused and inhaled sharply. His gaze sought hers. "Miss Stone . . . Bethany, would you consider coming with me?"

Chapter Two

The Moisant International Airport was a beehive of activity just as Bethany had expected it would be. The first thing Joshua did once they'd entered the terminal was check the flight schedule from the television monitor positioned beside the airline reservation desk.

"The plane's on time," he announced briskly, sounding as though he'd been hoping for a short reprieve. With his hand lightly touching Bethany's elbow, he hurriedly guided her through the wide corridor to the assigned concourse, despite the fact that they'd arrived almost forty minutes before Angie's flight was scheduled to land. In all the time Bethany had known Joshua, she'd never seen him more unsettled. When it came to matters dealing with his business, he often revealed so little emotion that it had become his trademark. Bethany watched him now, amazed and pleased.

Once they found the assigned gate, Joshua paced the area, his hands buried deep in his pant pockets. After several tense minutes, he parked himself beside Bethany at the huge floor-to-ceiling window and glared bleakly into the darkness.

"I really appreciate your coming with me," he said. "I haven't seen Angie in almost a year." He jammed his fingers through his hair and released a harsh breath. "Do you think she'll recognize me?"

"I'm sure she will." Bethany searched for something more to say that would reassure him but wasn't confident he would appreciate her efforts. Joshua Norris was a difficult man to interpret. She didn't know how far she dared tread onto this carpet of unexpected trust he'd laid before her.

A series of flashing lights glowed in the distance and Bethany felt Joshua tense beside her. She checked her wristwatch and noted the time. "It's too early for that to be Angie's plane."

Her employer nodded and seemed to relax.

"Joshua," she whispered, unable to keep herself from speaking, "everything's going to work out fine."

At the sound of his name, his troubled gaze shot in her direction, and he frowned. His eyes revealed surprise mingled with bewilderment. "No one's called me that since I was a boy."

Color exploded in Bethany's cheeks, working its way to her ears until she was certain they glowed with the heat. She'd always thought of him as Joshua, called him that in all her thoughts. The world knew him as J. D. Norris, but she'd found the initials too abrupt for the complex man she knew him to be. "I . . . won't do it again."

"It wasn't a reprimand . . . Bethany, but a statement of fact." He said her name as though it felt awkward on his tongue, yet as though he had recognized that she had a name other than Miss Stone. When he continued to stare at her for a long moment, Bethany had the impression he was seeing her for the first time. Briefly she wondered if he liked what he saw. She knew her clear delicate features robbed her of any classic beauty. Her eyes were a pale shade of blue, but not unlike a thousand others'. Her cheekbones were slightly high, her nose firm and straight. But she didn't possess any one feature that would distinguish her as a great beauty. Friends had called her cute, but that was about the extent of it. She was neither short nor tall, just average height—a description that sounded so terribly boring. She was contemplating this fact when she noted that if Joshua were to take her in his arms—fat chance of that—but if it were to happen, the top of her head would just brush against his jawline. All he would need to do was bend his head and kiss her and her lips would meet his without . . .

"Are Angie's grandparents traveling with her?" she asked, purposely diverting her thoughts. With some effort, she tore her gaze from his, her composure badly shaken by the brief encounter.

"No." Joshua abruptly shook his head and turned back to stare out the window. "It couldn't be helped. She's flying in alone."

"Oh." For a ten-year-old to be placed on a plane in New York to make this long trip by herself seemed almost irresponsible to Bethany, but she kept her opinion to herself. Poor Angie. With the time difference between the two cities, the little girl would probably be exhausted—or as keyed up and as full of energy as a fresh battery.

"Has her bed been made up?"

"Bed?" Joshua echoed the word as though it were something totally foreign. "I thought I'd put her in the guest bedroom for tonight... I hadn't stopped to think beyond that. I suppose she'll need something more, won't she?" His gaze clouded.

"I'm sure the guest room will be fine for now."

"Good."

A fresh set of wing lights blinked in the distant night. "I think that's her flight now," Bethany said.

Joshua stiffened, seeming to brace himself, and nodded. "She should be one of the first ones to disembark—I arranged for a first-class ticket."

"The flight attendant will probably escort her off."

Once again, Joshua gave a nonverbal reply, then exhaled sharply. "I can't tell you how glad I am that you're here with me."

Bethany couldn't have been more pleased herself. She'd been granted a glimpse of a whole new facet to Joshua Norris's personality. When it came to his daughter, he was a marshmallow. It seemed completely contradictory that this same man could bring a room full of board members to silence with one shattering look. She'd witnessed glares from Joshua that were colder than a tombstone in midwinter. No one would ever guess that the man who was nervously waiting for his young daughter was the driving force behind a thriving business. Bethany had trouble believing it herself.

An airline official opened the door to the jetway and two older businessmen were the first to step into the airport, carrying briefcases and garment bags. They were followed by a female flight attendant escorting a wide-eyed little girl with straight dark hair that fell to the top of her shoulders. Two pink ribbons held it away from her face, which seemed to be made up solely of round eager eyes.

"Daddy!" The girl broke away from the attendant and ran toward Joshua.

J. D. Norris looked startled, then fell to one knee as his daughter hurled herself into his waiting arms.

Two small arms flew around his neck and squeezed for all they were worth. Slowly, almost as if it were against his will, Joshua closed his eyes and returned the bear hug.

Bethany felt moisture brim in her eyes at the tender scene and bit into her bottom lip, determined not to say or do anything to disturb their reunion.

Finally Joshua released his daughter and stood, claiming her hand. "Angie," he murmured, looking down on the ten-year-old, "this is Miss Stone. She's my secretary."

"Hello." Wide dark eyes stared up at Bethany.

"Hello, Angie. Welcome to New Orleans."

"Thanks." The preteen grinned and let loose with an adult-sounding sigh. "I can't tell you how boring that flight was. I was beginning to think I'd never get here."

"I believe your father was feeling much the same thing."

Angie's smile grew wider. "I don't suppose there's a McDonald's around here. Grandma told me not to trust anything the airlines served and I'm absolutely starved."

"Miss Stone—a McDonald's?" Joshua was looking at her as though he expected her to wave a magic wand so one could instantly appear.

"Any hamburger will do," Angie offered next, her gaze growing wide and desperate.

"There's a McDonald's a few miles away."

"Thank goodness," the little girl sighed, shrugging her small shoulders. "I swear I could eat one of everything they have."

Come to think of it, Bethany hadn't had dinner yet, either. Her stomach growled eagerly at the mere mention of a Big Mac.

Angie prattled on about New York and her grandparents as they moved down the concourse to the baggage claim area. In addition to the carry-on bag the little girl had with her, there were three large suitcases.

Once they were seated inside Joshua's car, Angie leaned over the seat so her head was positioned between Bethany and Joshua.

"You're a winter, aren't you, Miss Stone?"

"A winter?" She hadn't a clue what the ten-year-old was talking about.

"Your coloring—haven't you ever been analyzed?" She smothered a yawn with her palm. "It was the latest thing a few years back."

"I guess I must have missed that."

"You needn't have it done now. I have a gift for these things, and you're definitely a winter," Angie returned confidently. "You should wear more bright clothes—reds, blues, whites, those sort of colors."

"Oh." Bethany wasn't sure how to comment. As it was, her wardrobe consisted of several bold colors, but she wore more subdued ones for the office—tans and soft blues mostly.

"Cheryl Tiegs, the model, has got a wonderful program on the Arts and Entertainment channel. You should watch that for a few fashion hints."

"Yes," Bethany said, hiding a grin. "I suppose I should."

"How's the sailing going, Dad?"

"Good," Joshua said distractedly. He seemed more concerned with getting out of the heavy airport traffic at the moment.

"I saw an interview with some guys on the sports station last night. You might think about studying tacking techniques if you want to be a really great sailor. Personally, I think the New Zealanders are the ones we're going to have to watch in the next America's Cup."

"That could very well be true." Joshua's smiling gaze bounced off Bethany's as he briefly rolled his eyes.

Angie crossed her arms over the seat and pressed her chin on top of her folded hands. She hesitated for a quick moment, then said, "We're going to get along just fine, don't you think?"

"Just fine," Joshua echoed. "What I'd like right now, though, is for you to sit back and buckle up the way you're supposed to."

Bethany sucked in her breath. His words were clipped and far more harsh than necessary. Joshua was right, but there were gentler ways of telling his daughter so.

"Oh, sure." Angie immediately obeyed, flopping back against the car seat and slipping the seat belt neatly into place. "You should have done this years ago."

"Done what?" Joshua's question was absent as he pulled to a stop to pay the attendant the parking fee.

"Sent for me," Angie said on the tail end of a yawn.

Joshua didn't answer her for what seemed like an eternity. "You may be right," he murmured at last.

Bethany noted how his face eased into a relaxed smile. It struck her then how rare it was for Joshua Norris to show pleasure at something. He ran a tight ship as the saying went. He lived his life according to a rigid schedule, driving himself and everyone who worked closely with him to the brink of exhaustion. The control with which he molded his existence was bound to change now that his daughter had arrived. For the better, Bethany dared to hope. For the better.

Bethany curved her fingers around the purse that rested on her lap. The letter of resignation neatly folded inside would stay there. Exciting things were about to happen at Norris Pharmaceutical and with J.

D. Norris, and Bethany planned to stick around and witness each one.

The living room drape was pushed aside and Sally's eager face was reflected in the glass when the taxi deposited Bethany in front of her apartment two hours later.

"It's about time you got home," Sally cried the minute Bethany walked inside the door. "What happened? I've been dying to talk to you. Good grief, girl, you should have phoned." She inhaled a huge breath and sank onto the thick sofa cushion. "But don't worry about apologizing now. Talk."

Bethany hung her jacket in the hall closet, biding her time. She wasn't exactly sure where to start. "Mr. Norris followed me out of Charley's..."

"I know that much. Good heavens, what did he say to you? I don't know when I've seen you look more...I don't know...stricken, I guess."

"That doesn't matter."

"He followed you, though?"

"Yes. He told me his daughter is coming to live with him."

Sally folded her pajama-clad legs under her and leaned back, her look thoughtful. Twin brows arched speculatively as she bounced her finger over her closed lips several times. "Well, that's news."

"Angie arrived tonight, and Mr. Norris asked me to go to the airport with him."

"So that's where you've been?"

"Part of the time." Bethany slipped off her low-heeled shoes and claimed the overstuffed recliner across from her roommate. "After that we went to McDonald's."

Sally grinned at that, her smile slightly off center. "How romantic."

Actually it had been, but she wasn't about to explain that to her friend. Bethany was convinced it was the first time Joshua had ever been to a fast-food place, and he'd looked as uncomfortable as a pond fish during a summer drought. "We went through the drive-in window because it was obvious Angie was going to conk out any minute."

"And did she?"

"The poor kid was fast asleep by the time we arrived at his house."

"You saw Mr. Norris's house?" Sally uncrossed her legs and leaned forward. They'd once heard that Joshua lived in a mansion.

Bethany answered with a short nod, remembering her first impression of the breathtaking beauty of the two-story colonial building. The antebellum home was constructed of used brick in muted shades of white and red. Four white gables peeked out stately from the roof line above the second floor. The front of the house was decorated with six huge brick columns that were lushly covered with climbing ivy. Joshua's home was a tasteful blend of the old South and her warm traditions with the new South and her willingness to adapt to change.

"What happened there?" Sally pressed, unable to hide her curiosity.

Bethany answered with a soft shrug. "Angie was asleep by the time we arrived, so while I helped her undress and get ready for bed, Mr. Norris brought in her luggage.''

"And?"

"And then he phoned for a taxi so I'd have a way home."

He'd also thanked her and apologized once more for his behavior earlier that evening. And as he did, Bethany noted that he was closing himself off from her again. She could see it as clearly as if she were standing before a huge gate that was mechanically being shut. She tried to read his features, but it was impossible. She suspected that he'd regretted having confided in her once the crisis had passed, and that hurt just a little.

Bethany didn't mention any of this to Sally, nor did she tell her roommate how Joshua had walked her to the cab once it arrived and paid her fare. He'd lingered outside a few moments, hands buried deep in his pant pockets, his face lined with a frown that left Bethany brooding all the way home.

"That's it?" Sally asked, looking sadly disappointed. "You were gone for hours and that's the extent of what happened the entire time?"

"That's all there was." On the surface it didn't sound like much, and really it wasn't, but far more had been accomplished. So much more than Bethany had ever dared to hope in a long while. For the first time since she'd been hired as J. D. Norris's personal secretary, her employer had seen her as something more than an automaton. She chose to think he was pleasantly surprised by what he'd found.

Bethany was at her desk by the time Joshua arrived on Monday morning. She glanced up expectantly and was disappointed when he did nothing more than offer her a crisp good-morning the way he'd done every day of the past three years. He marched by her desk and into his office.

Reaching for the mail, Bethany followed him inside. She'd taken his daughter's advice and chosen a dark blue business suit with a white silk blouse and a ribbon tie. Briefly she wondered if Joshua would notice anything as mundane as the way she dressed. Probably not.

Following ritual, she poured him a mug of hot coffee and delivered it to his desk. Joshua reached for the brew and took a sip before quickly leafing through the mail. He gave brisk instructions on each piece, handed back the ones she could deal with directly and kept the rest. Once he'd finished, Bethany hesitated, standing beside his desk, uncertain.

"Yes?" he questioned crisply. "Was there something more?" He didn't so much as look up at her.

"I . . . wanted to ask you about Angie," she managed finally, having trouble getting the words past an uncooperative tongue. His facade was back, and from the hard look about him, it had been heavily reinforced.

"Miss Stone, in case you've forgotten, I have a business to run. My daughter is none of your concern. Now, may I be so bold as to suggest that you do the job for which I handsomely pay you?"

It took Bethany a moment to blink back the incredible hurt. "Yes, of course." Her voice was hardly more than a whisper. She found that her hands were trembling by the time she'd returned to her desk. Her legs weren't in much better shape.

By rote she managed to finish the morning's tasks, but by the time Sally arrived at noon, Bethany had worked herself into an uncharacteristic anger. She shook from the force of it, furious with herself for allowing Joshua to speak to her in that horrible tone as though she were his personal slave.

"He's impossible," she hissed when her friend stuck her head in the door.

"Mr. Norris?" Sally's gaze traveled in lazy perusal from her roommate to the closed door that connected the two rooms.

"Who else?" Bethany pushed back her chair so hard, she soared six feet from the desk.

Frowning heavily, Sally stepped into the office. "Good grief, what happened?"

"I've had it!" Bethany declared, and cringed when Sally rolled her eyes toward the ceiling. Okay, so she'd been saying the same thing for weeks, but today was different. She would show Joshua Norris that she was a woman with emotions and feelings, deserving respect. She refused to allow any man to talk to her the way J. D. Norris had. Never again. The worm had developed a backbone at last.

She reached for her purse and headed toward the door.

Openmouthed, Sally lingered behind. "Aren't you going to let the great white hunter know you're leaving?"

"No. He'll figure it out for himself."

Sally closed her mouth, then promptly opened it again. "Okay."

Bethany was halfway out the door when she glanced over her shoulder at Joshua's office. A great sadness settled over her heart and she inhaled a soft sigh of regret. Her relationship with J. D. Norris seemed to be one step forward followed almost immediately by two giant leaps back. She'd been given a rare glimpse of the man she knew him to be and feared she was destined to wait a lifetime to be granted another peek.

Unusually quiet, Sally led the way to the company cafeteria on the third floor. They ordered their lunch, then carried the bright orange trays to the round table by the window that overlooked the rambling Mississippi River.

"You're right, you know," Bethany spoke first. "I should have quit long before now." Like a romantic schoolgirl, she'd believed that the love of a good woman would be enough to change Joshua. But she was wrong. He didn't want her love, didn't need her. Their time together with Angie was an embarrassment to him now, something he obviously regretted.

"I'm right about what? J. D. Norris?" Sally asked, watching her friend carefully. When Bethany didn't respond right away, she peeled open her turkey-on-wheat sandwich to remove the lettuce. She reached for the salt shaker in the middle of the table, then changed her mind and replaced it.

A long minute passed before Bethany nodded.

"Well?" Sally demanded. "Are you going to spill your guts or not?"

"Not," Bethany answered in a small voice that was filled with regret. She couldn't explain to Sally facts she herself had only recently faced. She had been pining away for three good years of her life, and just when she'd been given a glimmer of hope, she'd been forced to recognize how futile the whole situation was.

Eventually Sally would wear her down, Bethany realized. Her friend usually came up with some new way of drilling the information out of her. But she wasn't ready to talk yet. She lifted her pastrami sandwich from the plate and realized she might as well have been contemplating eating Mississippi mud for all the appeal her lunch held. She returned the sandwich, untouched, to the plate and pushed it aside.

"You realize I've heard all this before."

"Of course I realize that. But this time is different."

"Right," Sally said with a soft snicker.

"No, I really mean it," Bethany returned. "Listen, I recently read that the best time to find a job is when you're currently employed. I'm going to start applying for a new position first thing tomorrow morning."

Sally's narrowed gaze said that she wasn't sure if she could believe her friend or not. Bethany met that look with a determination that had been sadly absent in the past. This time she meant it—she honestly meant it. She was leaving Joshua Norris for good.

When Bethany returned to the office, the morning paper tucked under her arm, Joshua's door was open. He must have heard her because he stepped out and stood at her desk for a moment. Although she refused to meet his gaze, she could feel him assessing her. He left without a word a couple of minutes later.

The instant he was gone, Bethany spread open the newspaper to the want-ads section, carefully read the help-wanted columns and made two calls, setting up appointments.

An hour later Joshua returned, but he didn't speak to her then, either, which was just as well.

The afternoon passed quickly. Joshua requested two files and dictated a letter, which Bethany typed and returned within the half hour. No other communication passed between them, verbal or otherwise.

Once more Joshua left the office for a meeting with accounting, and fifteen minutes later Bethany walked out to meet Sally for their afternoon coffee break. Sally apparently had decided to keep her opinions to herself, because the subject of J. D. Norris didn't come up.

When Bethany returned to the office, she decided she'd ask Joshua for Thursday morning off. She would tell him she had an appointment, which was true. The appointment was to fill out job applications. And next time she accepted a job, she was going to be certain that her employer was happily married and over fifty.

"Miss Stone. Hi."

Bethany's gaze flew to her desk, where Angie sat waiting.

The youngster jumped up and smiled, looking pleased to see Bethany again. "I didn't think you'd ever get back."

"Hello, Angie." The little girl's welcoming smile would rival a Louisiana sunset. "How was your first day of school?"

The ten-year-old wrinkled up her nose. "There are a bunch of weird kids living in this town."

"Oh?"

"Not a single girl in my class has ever heard of Bobby Short."

While gnawing on her lower lip, Bethany scanned her own repertoire of famous men's names and came up blank. "What a shame," she answered, hoping Joshua's daughter wouldn't lump her in the same category as the others.

"Anyone who knows anything about music must have heard about Bobby. Why... he's world famous. Grandma and Grandpa are personally acquainted with him. Once they took me to the Carlisle so I could hear him." She crossed her arms and gave a short little pout.

At the mention of the famous New York hotel, Bethany was reassured. Bobby Short was a singer.

"I'm not going to tell Dad this," Angie continued, her voice dropping to a soft whisper, "because it would upset him, but my fellow students have no class."

Making no comment, Bethany deposited her purse in the bottom desk drawer and took her chair.

Angie came around the other side of the typewriter to face her. "Do you like Madonna?"

Containing a smile was impossible. "Quite a bit, as a matter of fact."

The youngster seemed surprised that Bethany would openly admit as much. "I do, too, but Grandma claims she's a hussy."

"And what does that mean?" The laugh worked its way up Bethany's throat but was quickly closed off when her gaze met a dark, serious pair of brown eyes.

Angie shook her head. "I'm not sure, but I think it has something to do with the fact Madonna has pierced ears."

Bethany sincerely hoped the ten-year-old hadn't noticed her ears. God only knew what she'd think of someone who had each lobe pierced *twice*. To divert the child's attention, she rolled a piece of paper into her typewriter.

Angie wheeled a chair to the side of Bethany's desk. "Dad said I'm not supposed to bother you when you're working. The new housekeeper can't come until tomorrow and so I'm here for the afternoon."

"You won't be a bother, sweetheart."

Angie looked relieved at that. "What are you doing now?"

"I'm about to type a letter for your dad."

"Can I watch?"

"If you want." Bethany's fingers dexterously flew over the keys. She finished within a few minutes.

"You're good."

"Do you want to try?"

If Bethany had thought the youngster's eyes were round before, now they resembled black orbs. "Can I really?"

In response, Bethany placed a fresh sheet of paper in the machine and moved aside. "It's all yours."

For the next hour Angie became Bethany's shadow. The little girl was a joy, and more than once Bethany was unable to hold back a laugh. Angela Norris was unlike any ten-year-old Bethany had ever known. Despite the fact that she'd been raised by her grandparents and had attended a small private school, Angie appeared utterly unspoiled. Bethany found that fact remarkable.

It was nearly five o'clock by the time Joshua returned from his meeting.

"Hi, Dad," Angie greeted. "Bethany let me use her fingernail polish. See." She held up both hands, revealing pink-tipped fingers.

The phone rang before Joshua could respond.

"I'll get that."

Bethany sucked in her breath as Angie reached for the receiver. "Mr. Norris's office, how may I help you?"

"Miss Stone?" Joshua arched his brows in a disapproving slant. "Is this your doing?"

Bethany's response was to offer him a weak guilty smile.

Angie pressed the telephone receiver to her shoulder and looked at Bethany. "It's someone named Sally asking for you."

Joshua's gaze sliced into Bethany, condensed with disapproval. "As soon as you're finished, Miss Stone, I'd like to see you in my office."

Chapter Three

Y ou wanted to see me, Mr. Norris?'' Bethany asked in a brisk businesslike tone, devoid of emotion. She trained her gaze on a point on the wall behind him so she needn't subject herself to his cool assessing eyes. No doubt she'd done something more to displease him. Again. It wasn't as though she hadn't been trying. All day she'd been finding petty ways of getting back at him for his cold treatment of her earlier in the day. Bethany didn't like to think of herself as a mean-minded person, but working with Joshua had reduced her to this level. It was more than enough reason to find other employment.

"I wanted to apologize for Angie being here," he said.

Bethany relaxed. "She hasn't been a problem, sir."

"Good. The housekeeper I hired starts tomorrow, so this will be the last time Angie will need to come to the office."

"I understand." Although it required some will, Bethany kept her gaze centered on the landscape drawing behind Joshua. "Will that be all?"

"Yes." He sounded hesitant.

Bethany did a crisp about-face and marched with military precision toward the door. She paused when she remembered her plan to look for another job. "Mr. Norris?"

"Yes?"

"I'll need Thursday off."

"This Thursday?"

"If . . . if it wouldn't be too much of an imposition. I've got an appointment."

"For all day?"

She straightened her shoulders. "That's correct."

He didn't sound pleased, but that wasn't Bethany's problem. "All right, Miss Stone, arrange for personnel to send me a substitute, then."

"Right away, sir."

"Miss Stone," he called out impatiently, his tone angry. "Kindly drop the 'sir,' will you? You haven't used it in the past and it's unnecessary to call me that now. Is that understood?"

"Perfectly, Mr. Norris."

Joshua expelled his breath in what sounded like a frustrated sigh. "Miss Stone, is there a problem?"

Bethany turned to him, keeping her face as devoid of emotion as possible. "What could possibly be wrong?'' she asked in as much of a singsong sarcastic voice as she dared without invoking his full ire.

"That's my question!" he shouted.

"Then that's my answer."

His eyes rounded with surprise and he looked as though he wanted to say something more. But when he didn't speak immediately, Bethany turned and quickly left the room. She'd never spoken to Mr. Norris that way, never once revealed any of what she was thinking or feeling for fear she would say or do something to cause his displeasure. She hadn't dared. But she wouldn't be in Joshua Norris's employment much longer and the sense of freedom she felt amazed her.

"Miss Stone?" Angie asked, her wide eyes studying Bethany. "Is my dad mad at you?"

"No, honey, of course not."

"Good." The little girl released a long sigh that seemed to deflate her posture until her small shoulders sagged with relief. "He has a habit of saying things in this deep dark voice that scares people. It used to make me want to cry, but then I realized he talks that way most of the time, and he isn't really mad."

"I know, Angie. If you'd like, you can call me Bethany."

"I can?"

"But only if we can be friends."

The ten-year-old released another one of those balloon-whooshing sighs. "After the day I've had, believe me, I could use one."

Bethany laughed outright at that, unable to stop herself, although she could see that the little girl was dead serious.

"It's true," Angie murmured, her dark eyes round and sad. "I don't think anyone in my new class likes me. I'm not sure what I did wrong, either. But I think Grandma would say I was trying too hard."

"Give it time, sweetheart."

Angie nodded and grinned. "That's something else Grandma would say."

"By the end of the week you'll have all kinds of new friends."

"Do you honestly think so?"

Bethany gave her a reassuring nod and rolled a clean piece of paper into her typewriter. "How would you like to type a letter for me?"

"I can do that?"

"Sure. I've got some filing to do, and since you're here, you can be my personal assistant." She laid a form letter on the tabletop for the little girl to copy.

"I'll do my best, Miss Stone. I mean . . . Bethany." Angie slid the chair toward the typewriter, looking as efficient and businesslike as possible for a preteen.

Within a couple of minutes, Angie's brow was folded with concentration as her fingers went on a seek-and-find mission for each typewriter key. It took the girl an hour to finish the few short sentences of the letter, but when she was done, Angie looked as proud as if she'd climbed Stone Mountain unaided.

"You did a fine job, Angie," Bethany told her, glancing over the finished product.

"Oh hi, Dad," Angie said, flew off her chair and went running toward her father. "Guess what? Bethany said I can be her personal assistant. I can come back tomorrow, can't I? You aren't really going to make me stay with that stuffy old housekeeper, are you? Bethany needs me here."

Bethany opened her mouth, then closed it. Oh, dear, she'd only been trying to amuse Joshua's daughter, and now it looked as though she'd created a problem instead of solving one.

"There may be an occasional afternoon when Miss Stone could use your help," Joshua admitted thoughtfully, his gaze resting on Bethany. "But Miss Stone is quite efficient, so you shouldn't count on coming every day."

"But, Dad . . ."

"My secretary is usually able to handle all the work herself," Joshua said, interrupting the little girl in a voice that brooked no argument.

"I *want* to help her, though. As often as I can, and I should be able to come every afternoon, don't you think, Bethany?"

"I said you may come occasionally," Joshua reiterated, "and that's all the argument I'm willing to listen to, Angela."

"Yes, Daddy." She didn't look pleased, but she wasn't completely deflated, either.

Considering everything, Bethany felt Joshua had offered a decent compromise. When she left the office that night, Bethany realized she was actually pleased with the way her employer had handled the situation with his daughter. He may not have had a lot of opportunity to do much parenting, but he seemed to be adapting nicely. Angie and Joshua would get along fine without her. At least, that was what Bethany kept telling herself.

Thursday afternoon, Bethany was sitting in front of the television, her feet propped up on the coffee table and a hot drink cupped in her hand, when her roommate let herself into the apartment.

"You look like you had a rough day," Sally commented.

"It's a jungle out there," Bethany said forcefully. Her feet ached, her spirits sagged, and she wondered if there would ever be a job that would free her heart from Joshua Norris.

"I take it a fantastic job didn't plop itself down in your lap?"

"The woman's a mind reader."

"What happened?"

"Nothing, unfortunately," Bethany admitted with a soft moan of discouragement. "I left my application in with ten different companies and was interviewed for positions with two others. I got the old 'don't call us, we'll call you' routine."

"What are you going to do?" Sally asked, the concern in her voice evident with each syllable.

"What else can I do?" Bethany answered. "I'll stick it out with Joshua Norris until I find something suitable."

Her friend plunked herself onto the sofa beside Bethany and raised her feet onto the coffee table. "Well, I've got news for you, too."

"What?" Bethany was in the mood for something uplifting.

"Apparently Mr. Norris didn't have a good day without you."

"Oh?"

"He went through two substitutes before noon."

"Good grief, who did personnel send him?"

"I don't know, but the word was, Mr. Norris was in a foul mood all day."

Bethany tugged at the corner of her lower lip with her teeth. "I wonder why?"

"So does everyone else. I'll tell you one thing, though. There isn't a secretary in the entire company who isn't glad you're coming back tomorrow morning. Every one of them spent an anxious afternoon fearing they were going to be sent to work in Mr. Norris's office. It's like ordering a vestal virgin to walk into the dragon's den."

"He's not that bad!" Joshua might have faults, but he certainly wasn't a tyrant. Bethany wouldn't have fallen in love with a slave driver.

"Mr. Norris isn't bad? Wanna bet?" Sally returned forcefully. "Rumor has it that J. D. Norris told the first secretary she was a complete ninny."

Bethany gritted her teeth to keep from defending Joshua. It was apparent to her, if not to her roommate, that if her employer called her replacement a ninny it was highly probable that the woman had done something stupid. Bethany didn't know who personnel had sent up to replace her, but it seemed the problem lay with them and not her employer.

"You are planning to go back tomorrow, aren't you?" Sally asked expectantly.

Bethany nodded; she didn't have any choice but to return. She'd envisioned walking into his office and slapping down her two-week notice, all the while smiling smugly at J. D. Norris. But that wouldn't be impossible.

"Having you return in the morning is going to save me a good deal of telephoning."

"Telephoning?"

"Yeah," her roommate said, looking pleased. "I promised I'd call the others and let them know if you weren't going to work, because in that case, every secretary in the company was planning to call in sick."

"But that's ridiculous."

"You weren't at the office today, Beth. You couldn't possibly know what rumors have been circulating. I swear there isn't a woman in all Norris Pharmaceutical who doesn't think you should be nominated for sainthood."

Bethany grinned at that. It did her ego a world of good to have others think of her as irreplaceable. Unfortunately, Joshua was the only one who mattered, and he didn't seem to care one way or the other what happened to her.

The following morning proved her wrong.

Bethany was at her desk when Joshua strolled into the office. He paused just inside the door and looked relieved when he saw her sitting there. It may have been the lighting, but Bethany thought she saw his gaze soften. A brief smile touched his mouth; of that, she was sure.

"Good morning, Bethany."

"Mr. Norris." She stood and was halfway into his office when she realized he'd called her by her first name. Her heart ping-ponged against her breast in glad reaction. For the first time in years she was a real person to Joshua and not some kind of motor-driven robot.

By the time she delivered a cup of freshly brewed coffee to his desk and handed him the mail, she'd managed to compose herself and wipe the last traces of jubilation from her face, but not from her heart. Never from her heart.

Joshua leafed through the correspondence and gave his instructions the way he did each weekday morning. When he was finished, however, he paused.

"Miss Stone?"

She'd already stood when he gestured for her to sit down again.

"Yes?"

"How long have you been working for me now? Three years?"

Bethany nodded.

"When was the last time I gave you a raise?"

"Four months ago." Her generous salary was part of the problem in finding another suitable position. Once she listed her current wages, most places were unwilling to meet or match her price. At least that was what Bethany surmised from her experiences the day before.

"You've done an excellent job for me, Miss Stone."

"Thank you."

"I tend not to tell you that often enough."

As Bethany recalled, he'd never said it, certainly not directly.

"We seem to work well together. Until you were gone yesterday I didn't realize how much you do to keep this office running smoothly."

"Thank you." She knew she sounded as if her vocabulary were limited to those two words, but he'd taken her by complete surprise and she couldn't find anything else to say that made any sense. There must have been some truth to what Sally had told her about her replacements, but Bethany had been absent from work more than once. Not often, but a day or two now and again.

"You anticipate my needs," Joshua went on to say, looking slightly embarrassed. "You seem to know what I'm thinking and act on it without my having to comment. I'm coming to realize that's a rare quality in an employee."

"Thank you." Her lack of ability to make brilliant or any other kind of conversation greatly chagrined her.

"I feel it would only be fair to compensate you for a job well done." He paused and looked pleased with himself.

"I beg your pardon." Bethany wasn't sure what he meant.

"I'm giving you another raise."

He mentioned a sum that made Bethany gasp. The amount was nearly twenty-five percent of her already more than adequate salary. "But I just received a wage increase last October."

Joshua arched his brows speculatively. "Does that mean you don't want this one?"

"Of course I want it."

"Good," he said briskly, turning his attention to the papers on his desk, dismissing her. "That will be all, then."

"Thank . . . you, Mr. . . . Norris," she said, coming awkwardly to a stand. A couple of the envelopes she was holding nearly slipped from her fingers, but she managed to grab them before they fell to the floor.

He grinned, and his look was almost boyish. "I believe you've adequately thanked me, Miss Stone."

Bethany couldn't return to her desk fast enough. The first thing she did was call Sally, who worked in the accounting department.

"Sally," she cried under her breath. "Meet me for coffee, okay?"

"Now? Bethany, dear, in case you haven't noticed, it's barely after eight."

"Not now, at ten, like always."

"Bethany?" her friend muttered, sounding vaguely concerned. "We've been meeting for coffee every day at ten for three years. Why would today be any different?"

"I got a raise!" Bethany cried, unable to hold the information inside any longer.

"Another one?"

To her way of thinking, Sally didn't sound nearly as pleased as she should have been. "What you said about yesterday must have been true, because Mr. Norris seemed more than pleased to see me this morning."

"Beth, does this mean you won't be looking for another job?"

"Are you nuts? Where else would I ever make this kind of money?"

"Where else would you risk breaking your heart?" Sally asked.

The question echoed through Bethany's mind like shouts bouncing off canyon walls. The reply was equally clear: nowhere else but with Joshua Norris.

Two weeks passed, and although nothing had actually changed, everything was different. There didn't seem to be any one thing that Bethany could pin down, but she felt more at ease with Joshua. Their routine remained exactly as it had been for three years, but Bethany intuitively recognized that Joshua felt more content. He was less formal, less austere. She guessed that the changes had come about as a result of having Angie come live with him. The ten-year-old was such a precious child that Bethany knew Joshua couldn't be around his daughter and not be affected.

Bethany was hungry for news of the little girl, but she dared not topple this fragile peace between her and her employer after that first morning when Joshua had made it clear that he didn't wish to discuss his daughter.

"Miss Stone?" Joshua called for her when she returned from her lunch break Friday afternoon.

Bethany reached for a pad and pencil and stepped into his office.

Joshua was leaning back in his chair, his hands forming a steeple that held up his chin; his look was thoughtful. "How much do you know about teen fashions?"

"Teen fashions?" she repeated, not certain she'd heard him correctly.

"Yes. Angela recently informed me she's 'out of it' and seemed quite concerned. Apparently not wearing the latest fad is a fate worse than death."

Bethany smiled and nodded, remembering her own teen years. Ten seemed a bit young, but she could understand Angie's wanting to fit in with the other girls her age.

"Short of dying her hair orange and piercing her nose, I have few objections to the way my daughter dresses."

Bethany nodded. She didn't particularly agree with that statement, but it wasn't her place to share her opinions on the matter with Joshua.

He straightened and looked uncomfortable. "I was wondering if it would be possible for you to take Angie shopping. She specifically asked for you, and I don't mind admitting I know next to nothing about how kids dress these days. Naturally I'd pay you for your time. It would mean a good deal to Angie."

"I'd enjoy it immensely."

He sighed then and actually grinned. "You don't know how relieved I am to hear that. I had visions of Angela dragging me through the women's lingerie department."

The following morning, Bethany met Angie and Joshua in a local shopping mall. The minute Angie saw Bethany approach, she broke loose of her father's hand and came running toward her as though they hadn't seen each other in years.

"Bethany, hi. I didn't think you'd ever get here."

Surprised, Bethany glanced at her wrist. "Am I late?" According to her watch, she was a full five minutes early.

"It seemed to take you forever," the ten-year-old said.

"We've been here ten minutes," Joshua admitted with an off-center grin that took away five years.

He looked so good that Bethany had to force her gaze back to Angie. "I take it you're excited?"

"Do the Saints play football?" Joshua asked, referring to the New Orleans football team, which had just finished an exceptionally good season.

"Dad said the sky's the limit. Are you ready?" she asked, her face a study in eagerness. "I know I am."

"Good luck," Joshua said, and paused to look at his gold watch. "I'll meet you for lunch. Where would you suggest?"

Before Bethany could answer, Angie called out, "McDonald's."

"You game?" Joshua asked her, looking more amused by the minute. Bethany had trouble recognizing him as the same man she worked with five days a week. For the first time in memory, he wasn't wearing a suit but was dressed casually in slacks and a light sweater that accentuated his china-blue eyes.

"McDonald's? Sure!" The last time she'd visited the fast-food restaurant had been the night they'd picked up Angie from the airport. If Joshua was game, then so was she.

By one o'clock that same afternoon, Bethany was exhausted, and Angie was just hitting her second wind. The child seemed tireless—a born shopper. It amazed Bethany how selective the ten-year-old was about her clothes. Although they'd been in at least fifteen different stores, Angie had only chosen a handful of items. Mostly sweatshirts and acid-washed jeans and a couple of pairs of white tennis shoes. Bethany did manage to talk her into one dress and a pair of patent leather shoes, but anything frilly simply wasn't her, as Angie put it.

Joshua was sitting in a booth in McDonald's munching on a french fry when Angie and Bethany joined him.

"How's it going?"

"Bethany really knows her stuff," Angie announced, already reaching for her Big Mac. "I knew the minute you told me she was going to take me shopping that this day would be special, and it has been."

Bethany felt her heart constrict at the little girl's praise. If anyone was special, it was Joshua's precocious daughter.

Angie dabbed her french fry in the catsup and lowered her gaze to the tabletop. "I just wish I could see Bethany more often."

Neither adult spoke. Bethany gave her attention to her own hamburger, staring at it, knowing she couldn't have swallowed a bite had her life depended on it. Joshua became unusually quiet, as well.

"Miss Stone is busy, Angie. She has other friends."

"Why do you call her Miss Stone, Dad?"

"I don't have that many other friends," Bethany said quickly. "I'd enjoy seeing Angie more often."

Joshua's eyes drifted from one female to the next, his gaze bewildered, as though he weren't certain who he should answer first. It was clear from the way he looked that he felt outnumbered.

"I call her Bethany and I bet you could, too," Angie added. "Grandma told me it was all right to call an adult by their first name if they said it was okay. I bet Bethany wouldn't mind if you called her by her name instead of Miss Stone all the time. Gee whiz, you see each other every day."

"Yes, well, I suppose I could if Miss Stone didn't object."

"Of course I don't mind."

"And you should call Dad J.D. like everyone else," Angie continued, speaking to Bethany.

"She prefers Joshua," he explained, his eyes holding Bethany's briefly. He grinned.

"Joshua." Angie rolled the name over the end of her tongue as if the sound of it were something rich and rare. "I like that, too. When I was born, if I'd been a boy, what would you and Mom have named me?"

"David. It's my middle name."

"Not Joshua?" Angie sounded disappointed.

"Too confusing," her father explained.

"What made you decide on something like Angela?" the little girl asked, closely studying her father. She was so intent that she stopped eating, and a french fry hung limply in her hand, halfway to her mouth.

"You looked like a tiny angel when the doctor first showed you to me," Joshua explained, and his gaze softened as it rested on his daughter. "I suggested the name Angela Catherine to your mother."

Angie nodded, not looking overly pleased. "I wish you'd thought I looked like a Millicent."

"Millicent?"

"Perhaps a Guinevere."

"Guinevere?" It was Bethany's turn to become an echo.

"Or even better a Charmaine." Dramatically the ten-year-old placed her hand over her heart, gazed into the distance and heaved an expressive sigh.

"Charmaine?" Bethany and Joshua repeated, and glanced at each other.

"Oh, yes. Those names sound pretty and smart. Angie sounds . . . I don't know . . . ordinary."

"Trust me, sweetheart, the last thing you are is conventional."

From the way Angie's eyes darted down to the table, it was apparent she didn't understand Joshua's meaning.

"That's another way of saying ordinary," Bethany explained.

"I knew that!"

Once more, Bethany and Joshua shared a brief smile.

"Bethany is such a pretty name. I wouldn't have minded that name, either."

"Thank you. My father named me, too."

"He did?"

"Yes, and when I was ten I wanted to be called Dominique because it sounded sophisticated and mysterious. I used to make up stories where I was the heroine who saved all my friends from certain death."

"You did?" Angie's eyes were growing rounder by the minute. "What about you, Dad? Did you ever want to be called something else when you were ten?"

"No."

Bethany resisted the urge to kick him under the table. Even if it was true, there wasn't any need to squelch the game.

"I believe I was closer to eleven at the time," he answered thoughtfully. "I wanted everyone to call me Mordecai. I felt it was a name that revealed character. When I said it, I felt stronger."

"Mordecai," Angie repeated slowly. "I like that almost as much as Joshua. Oh, Dad, this is the most fun I've had since moving to New Orleans."

Joshua grinned, and the smile Bethany had felt was so rare only hours before looked almost natural.

"Dad, can Bethany come home with us? Please? I want to show her my bedroom and my new television set and everything. You don't mind, do you?"

Chapter Four

Come see my bedroom next," Angie insisted, dragging Bethany by the hand down the long hallway. "Dad had a lady come in and decide on my colors and everything...only, I wish..." She paused and glanced over her shoulder before adding, "I like lavender much better than this lemon yellow she wanted me to have."

Bethany paused in the doorway of the ten-year-old's room and swallowed a soft gasp. The bedroom was elaborately decorated with ornate French-provincial-style furniture. A huge canopy bed dominated the room, with a matching desk and armoire close by. Thick canary-yellow carpeting covered the floor and was used to accent a lighter shade of sheer priscilla drapes. The bedspread was crafted from the same flowery pattern as the window covering.

"Don't you think it's simply divine?" Angie asked in a falsetto voice that Bethany was sure was a mimic of the designer. Angie's wide gaze studied her father's secretary for a response.

It was all Bethany could do to nod. Yes, the room was lovely, but it didn't typify Joshua's daughter. The little girl who preferred acid-washed jeans and sweatshirts hadn't once been consulted regarding what she wanted in her bedroom. Bethany would stake her career on the fact. This room belonged to a soft, feminine, demure child, and Angie was direct, tomboyish and full of vitality and life.

"Look at this," Angie said, stepping around her to the armoire. She opened the top doors and revealed a television with a twenty-six-inch screen. "I can sit on my bed and watch TV as late as I want."

"What about bedtime?" Bethany wished she hadn't asked that. She may be curious, but it was better that she not know, realizing already that she was going to disapprove. And if she did, she was powerless to say or do anything about it.

"Dad claims I'll go to sleep when I'm tired, and I do." She flopped down across the mattress on her stomach, legs raised and crossed at the ankles. She reached for the remote control, held it out like a laser gun and pressed a button. "Sometimes I fall asleep, and then Dad turns it off for me before he goes to bed."

Bethany managed a weak nod.

"He's real busy after dinner," the little girl informed Bethany, her eyes round and a little sad. "He has a lot of work to do...reading papers and stuff like that. You know."

Bethany did. "What do you do while your father's busy working?"

"Oh, nothing much. I come to my room and watch TV. Sometimes I read."

"What about homework?"

"Oh, Mrs. Larson, the housekeeper, has me do that as soon as I get home from school," she said, and sighed expressively, working her shoulders. "Mrs. Larson's all right, but I wish she'd let me play with the other kids, and after class is the only time I can do that."

"Have you made new friends?"

"Sure, lots—just like you said I would."

Bethany patted the top of the little girl's head, pleased. At least that adjustment had seemed to come easily enough.

"As soon as I admitted I like Madonna all the girls knew I was with-it." She paused, pressed a button on the remote control and turned off the television. "The afternoon you let me paint my fingernails helped, too, I think." Her gaze dropped suggestively to her clear nails, and she let loose with a hopeful sigh and raised pleading eyes to Bethany.

"I think I just may have a bottle of that same polish in my purse. If it's all right with your father, we'll coat your nails again before I leave."

"Oh, Dad won't care," Angie said, flying off the bed and throwing her arms around Bethany's waist for a bear hug.

"What won't I care about?" Joshua asked, leaning against the doorjamb, looking relaxed and amused.

His eyes sought out his daughter then drifted, almost reluctantly, to Bethany. The dark warm look in his gaze did funny things to her equilibrium and she reached out to steady herself against the bedpost.

"You won't care, will you, Dad?"

"About what, sweetheart?"

"If Bethany paints my fingernails again."

"No," he murmured, his gaze continuing to hold Bethany's. "I think that would be just fine."

"Do you want to come outside and look at the patio next?" Joshua's daughter wanted to know, her voice raised and eager. "Dad wanted to buy me a swing set, but I told him I was too old for that kind of kid stuff." She rolled her eyes for effect, and it took all Bethany's self-control not to laugh outright.

Joshua led them to the patio off the family room and gestured toward the white wicker furniture for Bethany to take a seat.

"Would you care for something to drink, Miss Stone?"

Angie slapped her hands against her thighs in a small display of disgust. "Honestly, Dad, I thought you were going to call her Bethany."

"Old habits die hard," he said, clearly trying to appease his young daughter.

"I'll take a cola," Angie said, sitting beside Bethany, swinging her stubby legs.

"Bethany?"

"Iced tea, if you have it. Thanks."

He cocked one brow and grinned broadly, his eyes alight with mischief. "What, no mint julep?"

Bethany quickly averted her gaze to Lake Pontchartrain, whose waters lapped lazily against the sandy shore only a few yards away. Joshua was teasing her about the Friday night she'd approached him at Charley's, and she didn't know how to respond.

"I'll be back in a minute."

"Do you want to walk down to the water?" Angie offered, jumping to her feet and holding out her hand to Bethany.

Bethany nodded eagerly. She'd always loved the lake, and she was more than willing to escape Joshua for a few moments. Questions were pounding against the edges of her mind like children beating against a locked door. She'd hungered for so long to know Joshua better. She was just as anxious for him to like her. It was happening and suddenly she was afraid. Terrified.

Sally would be furious with her for not having a witty comeback when he'd suggested the mint julep. He was accustomed to sophisticated women who knew how to spar verbally. All Bethany did was blush uncontrollably and look away, fearing what he would read in her gaze. At this rate, Joshua would never think of her as a mature woman and with good reason. Every time he looked at her with those warm lazy eyes, Bethany felt light headed and dizzy.

Angie slipped off her sneakers and socks and tested the water with her big toe. "It's really warm."

The day itself was almost balmy, even though it was only a few days into February.

"Do you think it would be all right if we waded a little bit? I think it would." Angie answered her own question and stepped out into the water until she was up to her calves.

Bethany slipped out of her sandals and followed, letting the cool lake lap at her toes. It was probably a silly thing to do, but she didn't care. The impulse to enjoy the water was too strong to resist.

"I love this lake," Angie said wistfully. "Dad says we'll be able to swim in a couple of months if the weather is nice, and it should be. I only wish Dad would let me swim alone, but he says I can't unless he's with me."

"He's right," Bethany said forcefully, a little frightened by the thought of Angie in the lake without an adult close by. "Don't ever go in the water alone. It's much too dangerous."

"Oh, I won't, but I don't think Dad will ever want to go. He has too much work to do. All he does is work, work, work. I tried to talk him into reading his papers on the patio so I could play by the water, but he said no to that, too."

Bethany agreed. It would be much too easy to become involved in whatever he was studying and to forget about Angie.

"Your dad's right, honey."

"I knew you'd say that," she answered with a soft pout.

Bethany laughed, enjoying the warm breeze that mussed her hair about her face. The water felt cool and refreshing, and before she knew it, she had lifted the skirt of her soft pink dress and was almost knee-deep.

"Hey, look," Angie called excitedly, waving frantically toward the house. "Dad's watching us."

Bethany twisted around and answered Joshua's wave with one of her own. In her dreams she'd often pictured a scene where they stood together by the lake with the wind whispering gently around them. She wished he would come down by the waterside and make her dream a reality. If she hadn't known better, Bethany would have thought Joshua was thinking the same thing, because the smile left his face and his gaze captured hers, holding it, refusing to let it go. The tender look was enough to cause her pulse rate to soar.

Bethany wasn't sure what happened next, or how she lost her footing, but suddenly, unexpectedly, she was slipping. Her arms flew out in a desperate effort to maintain her balance and remain upright. She should have known if she was going to make a complete fool of herself it would be in front of Joshua Norris. By the time she hit the water, she'd accepted her fate.

"Bethany, Bethany, are you all right?"

Mortified beyond all reasoning, Bethany sat in the chest-deep water and buried her red-hot face in her hands, unable to answer Joshua's daughter.

"Daddy, Daddy, I think Bethany's hurt!"

Bethany heard Angie's shouts as the little girl ran toward the house. Knowing there was nothing to do but face Joshua, she stood, awkwardly at best, and walked out of the water. Her once pretty dress was plastered over her torso and thighs, the ends of her hair dripped water onto the tops of her shoulders. Bethany didn't question how her hair could be wet and her shoulders dry, but they were.

Joshua stood on the shore, his hands braced against his hips, and did an admirable job, Bethany thought, of not laughing. She was convinced if he so much as snickered, she would burst into tears.

"Well, Miss Stone, how's the water?"

"Fine, thanks," she said, and her voice came out an octave higher than normal.

"I've sent Angela for a towel."

Bethany nodded her thanks and rubbed her hands up and down her chilled arms. A puddle of water pooled at her feet, and if it had been in her power to disappear, Bethany would have done so gladly.

"Here, Dad," Angie said breathlessly, rushing onto the scene, her arms loaded with a drawerful of soft thick towels.

Joshua draped one across Bethany's shoulders and held it there momentarily. "Whatever possessed you to wade in the lake?" he asked in a low growl. "For heaven's sake, it's February."

"The water was warm." The excuse sounded weak even to her own ears. The women Joshua knew didn't give in to impulses like that; they were too mature for something so silly, she thought with self-derision.

"Bethany, honestly." He pressed his forehead against hers. "Come in the house before you catch your death of a cold."

"I . . . I think it'd be best if I just went home," she whispered, utterly miserable.

"Like this? Wet? You can't do that. I refuse to allow it."

She was willing to suffer any discomfort in order to flee, even if it sounded completely nonsensical. But Bethany knew better than to argue with Joshua, and she nodded obediently.

With his arm cupping her shoulder, he directed her toward the house. At loose ends and wanting to help in some way, Angie ran circles around the two like a frolicking puppy.

"Are you all right, Bethany?"

"She's fine, sweetheart."

"It's all my fault."

"Bethany doesn't blame you. It was an accident, and those sometimes happen." Again Joshua answered for her.

Not knowing what to say or do to calm the distraught child, Bethany held out her hand. It was immediately clasped by a much smaller one.

Joshua led her through a set of sliding glass doors at the other end of the house into what was obviously the master bedroom. Bethany hesitated, not wanting to drip water all over his pearl-gray carpet, but he urged her forward and into the large master bathroom.

"Take a warm shower," he ordered, but not unkindly or in the harsh voice she was accustomed to hearing from him. "Give Angie your wet things and I'll have Mrs. Larson put them in the dryer."

Nodding seemed a monumental task, but Bethany managed.

"When you've finished, slip into my robe." He pointed to the thick navy blue one that hung on the back of the door. "I'll have a hot drink waiting for you."

Again she answered him with a short nod. He left her then and closed the door.

"I feel just terrible," Angie wailed, close to tears. "You'd never have gone into the water if it hadn't been for me."

"Sweetheart, don't worry about it. I stumbled over my own two feet." She didn't mention that she'd been looking at Joshua at the time and daydreaming about things that were never meant to be.

Angie slumped down on the edge of the bathtub, looking mournfully sad. "I will always blame myself for this."

"I refuse to let you," Bethany said, her teeth starting to chatter. "If you do, then I'll be forced to keep my nail polish in my purse."

"Well, actually, now that you mention it," the ten-year-old said as she nonchalantly stood and walked to the door, "it really *was* all your own fault. Are you normally this clumsy?"

"Always," Bethany muttered, and turned on the shower.

When she was finished, both Angie and Joshua were sitting in the living room waiting for her. Bethany tightened the cinch on the thick robe which was so long on her that the hem dragged across the carpet. Her hair hung in limp strands about her face, and she felt as if she should stand on a street corner and beg for alms.

Joshua stood when he saw her coming and made an admirable effort not to smile.

"Don't you dare laugh," Bethany warned him under her breath, and at the same time reassured Angie with a grin. She didn't know what she would do to Joshua if he did, but she'd find a way to make him regret it.

"I wouldn't *dream* of laughing."

"Ha!"

"I'll pour you a cup of coffee."

She sat in a velvet wingback chair and accepted the cup and saucer from Joshua when he brought them to her. "Thank you."

"You're quite welcome."

Bethany had the distinct feeling he was showing his appreciation for giving him the single biggest laugh of his life.

The first sip of coffee seared its way down her throat and caused Bethany's eyes to widen at its potency. It was apparent the moment the liquid passed her lips that the brew had been liberally laced with whiskey.

"This is... Irish... coffee?" she stammered on a breathless whisper, having trouble finding her voice.

"I didn't want you to catch a chill."

"Dad was real worried about you," Angie piped in. "He said you were lucky you didn't swallow a fish."

Bethany's narrowed gaze sliced through her employer. How she wished she could say exactly what she was thinking!

"I've instructed Mrs. Larson to set the table for three this evening," Joshua added.

Bethany had no idea it was this close to dinnertime. "I can't stay," she said hurriedly. "Really, I must be getting home."

"You can't just leave," Angie said, her young voice tight with disappointment. "We're having pork roast and homemade applesauce and fresh peas. But you don't have to eat the peas if you don't want. Dad makes me, but he won't make you . . . at least, I don't think he will."

Joshua stiffened and strolled to his daughter's side, resting his hand on her small shoulder. When he looked at Bethany, his gaze was guarded. "Miss Stone might have a date this evening, Angie. We shouldn't detain her."

"I . . . I'm not meeting anyone," Bethany said quickly. She shouldn't have been so eager to let Joshua know that, but the truth was she rarely dated anymore. There was no reason to when she was already in love.

"Then you'll stay for dinner?"

Bethany's gaze fell to the steaming coffee. "All right," she said. She couldn't find an excuse not to, except that she'd hoped to salvage what remained of her pride. Not that there was much left—most of it had drowned in Lake Pontchartrain earlier in the day. What little she'd managed to hold on to had been shredded by Joshua's comment about her swallowing a fish!

"Oh good, you'll stay," Angie said gleefully. "Mrs. Larson's a terrific cook."

By the time the meal was served, Bethany's clothes were back from Mrs. Larson and she'd had time to blow-dry and curl her hair. She felt infinitely better.

"I'm starved," Angie announced, claiming the chair beside Bethany and carefully unfolding the linen napkin across her lap.

"Swimming does that to me, too," Bethany added.

The corners of Joshua's mouth quivered before he burst into a full rich laugh. Soon they were all laughing.

"Rare is the woman who can find humor in her own misadventures," Joshua announced, and his face was transformed by a careless smile.

Flustered, Bethany looked away, unable to hold his gaze any longer.

Before their meal was served, Joshua poured Bethany a glass of wine. She wasn't sure she should drink it on top of the laced coffee, but she didn't feel it would hurt. A second glass followed at the end of the meal.

Angie fell asleep on the sofa while Bethany and Joshua lingered over their second glass of wine in the living room. Candles cast flickering shadows across the wall and the light in the room was muted, creating an intimate feeling.

"I've enjoyed today," Joshua said.

"I did, too."

"I'm grateful, Bethany, that you were willing to take Angie shopping. It meant a good deal to us both. I want you to know I was serious about paying you for your time."

"Oh, don't, please. Being with Angie is a delight." She didn't add that spending her day with Joshua had been equally thrilling. He was a completely different person away from the office. Having his daughter move in with him had sanded away the rough edges of Joshua's personality. Bethany's gaze shifted lovingly onto the sleeping child. Knowing Angie had opened a door for Bethany that she thought would be forever closed to her. She was eternally grateful to the little girl.

"Angie really seems taken with you."

He said it as though he couldn't understand why, and Bethany darted her eyes to her glass of wine as the pain rippled over her in widening waves, like a pebble tossed in a pond. It hurt so much that she didn't breathe until her lungs ached and an uncomfortable feeling took control.

"That surprises you, doesn't it?" she asked, and her voice wobbled a little, although she struggled to steady it.

"What?"

"That . . . that anyone could be taken with me."

Joshua looked completely shocked. "Not in the least."

Bethany decided it was the wine that had given her the courage to talk to Joshua that way, question him. God knew she never had before . . . wouldn't have dared.

"You certainly can be a prickly thing," he added, frowning.

"Me?" That just went to prove how much attention he'd paid her over the years.

"I meant to compliment you when I said how much Angie liked you."

"I apologize then."

"Fine."

A throbbing silence followed, during which Bethany was convinced they were both searching for ways to bring the conversation back to an amicable keel.

"I suppose I should think about driving home," Bethany murmured, discouraged and distressed. The day had held such promise, and the evening had been a disaster. She should never drink wine. It went straight to her head and disassociated her tongue from her brain.

"Before you do, I'd like to ask another favor of you, if I may," Joshua said.

Once more Bethany could feel his reluctance, as though he didn't like to be in her debt. "I'd be happy to do anything for you . . . for Angie," she hurried to add.

"It's about Mardi Gras next week. Angie is looking forward to attending the festivities, and, well, you know my schedule better than anyone. Would you be willing to take her to the parade? I could meet you afterward, and we could have dinner, the three of us. That is, of course, unless you've got other plans. I certainly wouldn't want you to cancel a date with someone special."

"I'd love to take Angie to the parade."

Joshua nodded and grinned. "Bethany?"

"Yes?"

"*Is* there someone special?"

To tell him the only one who mattered in her life was her employer would have been ludicrous and Bethany had the good sense to resist.

"No...not lately." She didn't know why she tagged that comment on, but she did, for better or worse.

"I see."

Bethany wasn't sure what he read into her answer—or what there was to read. "You don't have to meet us for dinner if you'd prefer to make other plans," she blurted out, then snapped her mouth closed, hardly able to believe she'd made that offer. "I mean . . . well, if you'd rather meet 'someone special,' I'll understand."

Joshua rotated the stem of his wineglass between his open palms. "There hasn't been anyone for me, either," he said in a low, well-modulated voice. "Not lately, anyway." He raised his eyes to hers and grinned.

Bethany relaxed against the back of the chair and smiled, more relaxed with Joshua than she could ever remember being. She'd often imagined quiet romantic moments such as these with him. But she'd always felt it would have been impossible.

"More wine?"

"No," she answered, and shook her head. "I'd better not since I have to drive home yet."

"I'll take you."

Although the thought was tempting, it would only be an inconvenience for Joshua, and she would need to have Sally drive her over to pick up her car later. Knowing Sally, and what her friend would read into the action . . . no, that just wouldn't work.

"Thank you, but no, I'll drive myself."

"What do you think of Angela's room?" Joshua asked, and glanced proudly toward the hallway that led to the bedrooms.

Bethany wasn't sure how to comment. "It's very... yellow, isn't it?"

"You don't like yellow?"

"Oh yes, it's a favorite color of mine." When it came to Joshua Norris, a wide streak of it ran down the middle of her back!

"Then why do I hear derision in your voice?"

"No reason." She hated to lie, but it wasn't her place to tell him Angela would have preferred lavender.

"You know, Miss Stone, you don't lie the least bit convincingly."

"No, I suppose I don't."

"Now, tell me what you find so offensive about the very expensive bedroom I had made up for my daughter."

"You've certainly made it appealing with the television and the stereo." Bethany hoped that would appease him, but one look at his frowning gaze told her differently.

"Yes. I realize she may be a bit young to appreciate some of that equipment."

"I just think—" Bethany stopped herself in time, silently cursing the wine for loosening her tongue.

"You think what?"

"Never mind." She shook her head so hard the hair whipped across her face. She brushed her index finger across her cheek to free a maverick strand.

"Bethany, I wouldn't ask your opinion unless I wanted it." His eyes were unusually dark and solemn.

"I worry about her, that's all," Bethany said, scooting forward a little in her chair. "You've created her own world for her and I don't know that that's the best thing for a ten-year-old who's recently left the only home she's ever known."

"You think because I can afford to give her a television and a stereo—"

"That's not my objection," she interrupted heatedly. Now that she'd started, the floodgate of opinion couldn't be held back. "Angie needs to be introduced to *your* world. She's got to spend time with you—not by herself in front of her own television while you watch yours. When you come home at night, she has to feel that she's more important to you than reading some report."

Joshua looked shocked. "I see."

"I don't mean to criticize you, Joshua, really I don't. It's just that I care so much about...about Angie." Dear Lord, if she didn't shut up soon, she would give him more than one reason to fire her.

"Well, you've certainly given me something to think about."

Bethany stood. It would be better if she left, before she said something to embarrass them both.

"I'll walk you to your car," Joshua murmured thoughtfully when she reached for her purse.

He escorted her outside and opened the driver's door for her. Scant inches separated them, and Bethany moistened her dry lips, feeling the night air fill with tension. The silence seemed to vibrate between them.

"There's more to you than I ever realized," Joshua admitted. He reached out and touched her cheek, gently gliding his finger down the side of her jaw as though he were touching the most valuable thing in the world.

Bethany closed her eyes to the delicious sensation that overtook her like an unexpected weakness. Her pulse began to beat wildly. He was so close, so wonderfully close, she could feel the heat radiate from his body. She knew her lips had parted with expectation. She wanted him to kiss her more than she had ever desired anything in her life. With her eyes still closed, she raised herself on tiptoe.

With a groan, Joshua settled his mouth hungrily over hers. He kissed her until she was flushed and trembling, sliding his mouth back and forth lazily across her own, soaking in her softness, savoring her gentleness. And yet, he gripped her shoulders as though he wanted to push her away and couldn't find the will to do so. If it were up to Bethany he would go on holding and kissing her forever. It was as she'd always imagined it would be in Joshua's arms. Her whole body felt as though it were convulsing in shock waves of pleasure. If a kiss did this to her, she could only dream what making love would do.

With an indrawn breath and a shudder, Joshua dragged his lips from hers and took a step back. "Bethany," he whispered in a voice she barely recognized. "You'd better go."

She wanted to argue with him, lock her arms around his neck and tell him she didn't ever want to leave him, but that would be impossible.

"Thank you," he whispered, his voice still husky.

For one wild second, Bethany didn't know why he should thank her for anything. Then her mind cleared, and she realized he was talking about helping with Angie. If anyone should be grateful, it was her.

Joshua had just proven that dreams actually *do* come true. He'd proven it by taking her in his arms.

Chapter Five

Monday morning Bethany sat at her desk, her stomach a mass of nerves. The wine, she told herself, it had been the wine that had done all the talking to Joshua Saturday night. In retrospect it astonished her that she could actually have told her employer how to raise his daughter. Who in heaven's name did she think she was? Dr. Benjamin Spock?

She was a secretary. Good grief, the closest she'd ever come to mothering was burping her three-month-old niece. Sure she liked kids, got along well with them, but that didn't give her the right to wade into another family and start issuing decrees.

If the wine had been talking for Bethany, it had done the kissing for Joshua. She knew Joshua well enough to believe that when he walked into the office this morning, he would pretend Saturday night had never happened. He'd crossed the line, no doubt regretted it and would immediately step back, hoping she hadn't noticed—or had the good sense to forget.

Only Bethany would never forget being in Joshua's arms. It felt so wonderfully right and good. But instead of fulfilling a need, it had created an ever greater one. The innocent emotion she'd held against her breast and nurtured had blossomed, leaving her craving so much more.

The door opened and Bethany held her breath as Joshua stepped into the office. He didn't so much as glance in her direction, and Bethany felt as if someone had dropped a sledgehammer over her head. She was right. He regretted everything.

"Good morning, Miss Stone," he said tersely on his way past her.

Bethany closed her eyes and firmly gritted her teeth. It was worse than she'd thought. Not only did Joshua wish he hadn't kissed her, he was sorry she was in his employment.

Picking up the mail, Bethany reluctantly followed him into the executive suite, pausing long enough to place the sorted correspondence on his desk and bring him a cup of freshly brewed coffee.

Joshua leafed through the stack of letters, paused and glanced in her direction. "How are you feeling, Miss Stone?"

"Fine." From the way the one word slipped the tight constriction in her throat, it was a wonder he didn't call for a paramedic.

"Good. Then there were no lingering effects from your...swim the other night?"

"No...none—" she dropped her gaze so fast she nearly dislocated a disk in her neck "—except for a loose tongue. Mr. Norris, I feel positively terrible that I could have spoken to you in such a manner. How you raise your daughter is none of my concern, and I sincerely hope that—"

"Miss Stone, kindly sit down."

Bethany nearly missed the chair in her eagerness to do as he asked. Her hold on the pencil was so tense it was a credit to American craftsmanship that the wood didn't snap in two.

Joshua held the coffee mug in both hands and leaned back in his chair, his look contemplative. "Ah, yes, your advice regarding Angela had slipped my mind."

Oh, brother. He'd forgotten, and she'd gone out of her way to remind him! "It was the wine, you see," she said hurriedly. "I should never drink more than one glass and I'd had two when we spoke. If you'll remember, I drank the Irish coffee earlier...and I can honestly say I wasn't quite myself Saturday evening."

"I see," Joshua said with a frown. "So you have regrets? Well, that's understandable."

"Mr. Norris, you have to understand that under those circumstances...like on Saturday...sometimes my tongue murmurs things I have no intention of saying aloud."

The frown grew darker, his brows crowding together until the ledge over his eyes formed a straight narrow line. He stiffened, seeming to close her off completely.

Bethany hated when he did that, but she was powerless to do anything more than react. "I truly am sorry, Mr. Norris," she finished weakly, utterly defeated.

"I believe you've apologized sufficiently. Shall we deal with the mail now, or is there anything else you care to confess before we get down to business?"

"The mail . . . of course."

Fifteen minutes later, Bethany stood, her head buzzing. She didn't exactly know where matters had gone wrong, but nothing seemed right. Joshua was terse and impatient, issuing orders faster than she could write down his instructions. When he did look at her, his handsome face was devoid of expression.

Bethany stood in front of the door that connected their two offices. Gathering her courage, she hesitated and turned around. She held the dictation pad to her breast like a shield of armor, her eyes infinitely sad. "Mr. Norris . . . one last thing."

"Yes. What is it now, Miss Stone?" he barked impatiently.

"I don't regret *everything* about Saturday night," she admitted in a raspy whisper, wanting to clear away one misconception, even at the cost of her own pride. "I can understand why *you* would prefer to forget what happened, but I don't. I . . . I promise not to embarrass either of us by ever mentioning it again."

She hurried to escape then, not waiting for a response, but several minutes later, Bethany was stunned to hear her employer whistling.

At lunchtime, Bethany pressed the button of her intercom. "Mr. Norris, I'm leaving now."

"Miss Stone," he said hurriedly, "last year . . . did I do anything special for you for Secretary's Day?"

Bethany had to think about it. "I'm not sure. You had flowers delivered, I believe."

A soft snicker followed. "As I recall you ordered the roses on your own. I had little to do with it."

"We . . . we did discuss it. Briefly."

"It seems to me most employers take their secretaries to lunch? Is that right?"

"I'm not sure."

"Lunch appears to be the proper protocol. If that's the case, it seems I owe you a lunch. Are you free this afternoon?"

Bethany's mouth made troutlike movements, opening and closing several times.

"Miss Stone?"

"Yes, I'm free."

"Good, I'll be finished here in about ten minutes."

She released the intercom and sat there with her mouth gaping open for a full minute before reality settled in. Joshua Norris had requested her company for lunch.

Sally stuck her head in the door. "Hey, are you coming or not? I'm hungry!"

Words square-danced on the tip of Bethany's tongue, and when she couldn't get them to cooperate with her brain, she jerked around and pointed her thumb toward Joshua's door.

"You mean the jerk won't let you leave to eat lunch?"

Bethany shook her head wildly.

"What, then? Good grief, woman, you look like you're about to keel over. What did that monster do to you this time?" Sally walked into the room and planted her hands on Bethany's desk, her eyes afire with outrage.

"I'm taking Miss Stone to lunch," Joshua announced, standing in the open doorway. "Is that a problem, Ms. Livingston?"

Sally leaped back from Bethany's desk as though she'd been struck by lightning. "No problem. Not for me. Well, I guess I should be getting along now. Do enjoy your lunch, Bethany. It was good to see you again, Mr. Norris . . . sir."

"Good day, Ms. Livingston."

Bethany's friend couldn't get out of the office fast enough. "See you later," she said weakly, and waved, all but trotting across the floor.

Joshua leaned against the doorjamb, indolently crossed his arms and legs, his face amused. "So I'm a monster. I wonder who could have given Ms. Livingston that impression?"

Bethany stood and tightly clenched her eelskin purse to her side. "There have been times in the past, Mr. Norris, when the description was more than apt."

"Is that a fact?" He seemed to find the information more humorous than offensive. "Then I'd best repent my obnoxious ways. I made reservations at Brennan's."

"Brennan's," Bethany repeated in an excited whisper. She'd lived in New Orleans most of her life and had never eaten at the world-famous restaurant.

"You approve?"

"Oh, Joshua...Mr. Norris, I'm...I'm very pleased. Thank you."

Their table was waiting for them when they arrived. If Joshua thought she was going to order a dainty shrimp salad and a glass of iced tea, then he was in for a surprise. Her appetite had always been healthy and she started off by ordering an appetizer plate, a Cobb salad, and, for the main course, Buster Crabs Béarnaise, a Brennan's specialty.

"You don't mind, do you?" she thought to ask, after the waiter had left their table.

"Of course I don't. I can see you plan to make up for all the years I didn't take you to lunch."

He was teasing her, but Bethany didn't mind. "That's not it."

"My dear Bethany, just where do you plan to put all that food?"

"Oh, don't worry. None of it will go to waste. I've never had a problem with my weight. None of the women in my family do until after they get pregnant, or so my mother and sisters tell me. From then on, keeping their figures is a constant battle. So I plan to enjoy all the goodies while I can." Bethany knew she was chattering, but she couldn't stop herself. Already she felt light-headed and the wine hadn't been poured yet.

"So you want children?" Joshua asked, watching her with smiling eyes.

Bethany spread a thick layer of butter over the top of the crisp French roll. "Of course."

"You're not afraid it'll ruin your figure?"

Bethany shrugged, pleased he hadn't noticed how thin she was. "Actually, I'm pretty much of a toothpick. I'm looking forward to adding a few curves. I'm just hoping they'll form in the right places. However, with my luck, my thirty-six-inch bust is likely to sink to my waistline." She paused in shock, amazed at what she'd just said and hoping that Joshua wasn't affronted by her loose tongue.

Joshua chuckled at that, then his eyes grew warm and serious. "I don't think you need worry, Bethany."

"I hope not," she said, and paid close attention to her roll in an attempt to calm her heart rate. She knew she shouldn't try to read anything into their conversation, but she couldn't help it. Her guess was that Angie's mother hadn't wanted children, and consequently Joshua thought all women felt the same way. It took everything within Bethany not to announce that she would gladly bear his child. At her errant thoughts she decided to forgo the wine.

"I told Angie you'd be escorting her to the Mardi Gras festivities, and she's excited, to say the least," Joshua went on to say.

"I'm looking forward to it myself."

"You honestly enjoy my daughter, don't you?"

Bethany found that a strange question. "Yes. She's delightful."

Joshua added a teaspoon of sugar in his coffee and stirred it vigorously. "I gave some consideration to what you said Saturday night. You may be right about me shutting Angie out of my life. It isn't easy after living all these years alone. But I wanted to tell you that I appreciate your insight."

"You do?" Bethany fingered the tassel on the wine list. Maybe alcohol wasn't such a detriment to her thought processes after all. Maybe it was just the thing needed to burst this romance wide open.

"I'm making an effort to spend more time with Angie, and find myself enjoying her. I have you to thank for that."

Bethany nodded, more pleased than she could remember being about anything in a long while.

"Unfortunately, time is something of a premium in my life," Joshua added in thoughtful tones. "These next six months are crucial to the future of Norris Pharmaceutical. There's a great deal at stake."

Bethany watched him carefully. She knew there had been a takeover effort made by another pharmaceutical firm several months back and that it had taken everything Joshua had to hold off the other company. His business was small yet, but the potential for growth was good if managed properly.

"What I'm trying to say is that I'm not going to have the opportunity to be a proper father to my daughter. There just isn't going to be the time for it."

Bethany opened her mouth to tell him "time" had little to do with being a good father. All Angie required was to know he loved her and that she was important to him. She needed him to listen to her problems and occasionally to laugh with her.

"Angie hasn't stopped asking about you since that first afternoon she spent at the office before Mrs.

Larson, the housekeeper, arrived. She seems to like you better than anyone."

Bethany's smile grew more forced by the minute. So their luncheon date hadn't been an excuse to get to know each other better, as she'd imagined. It was a bribe—pure and simple. Joshua wanted her to baby-sit his daughter. No doubt he was willing to pay her handsomely to become a lonely ten-year-old's surrogate parent.

"I'm going to be busy for the next several weekends," Joshua continued. "And I was wondering if you'd be willing to entertain Angela for me. Naturally I'd be more than happy to pay you for your time."

"Naturally," Bethany repeated.

The waiter delivered the appetizer tray and Bethany knew she wasn't going to be able to down a single bite.

"I'm such a fool," Bethany sobbed, holding her index finger under each eye in a fruitless effort to stop the flow of tears. Joshua had started asking her about children and keeping her figure, and like an idiot, Bethany had thought . . . had hoped that he'd become so enamored with her that he had marriage in mind. In her lovesick mind she'd pictured the two of them starting their own family. The humiliation of her silly, childish assumptions was almost more than she could bear.

"I can't believe I'd be so stupid," she wailed to Sally, who stood faithfully close by, a box of tissues firmly clenched in her hand. Bethany hadn't told her friend what had happened, couldn't bring herself to repeat what Joshua had asked of her over lunch, because it showed what a romantic fool she really was.

"Honestly, Beth, no amount of money is worth this agony," Sally said, handing her yet another tissue.

Bethany hiccuped a sob. "But I can't quit now."

"Why not?"

"Angie needs me."

"J. D. Norris is using his daughter to blackmail you into remaining his secretary? No wonder you're so upset!"

Bethany wiped her face free of moisture. "It isn't exactly blackmail," she said miserably. But the one who would suffer if she was to refuse to look after his daughter would be Angie. The ten-year-old had endured enough turmoil in the past few weeks. Okay, if Joshua was planning on using her to keep his daughter occupied and out of his hair, Bethany would do it. But she had learned her lesson when it came to her employer. She was going to guard her heart well. She was completely unwilling to be made a fool a second time.

"At least tell me what horrible things he did," Sally cried, growing more impatient when it became obvious that Bethany wasn't going to let her know anything but the basics. "If you tell me what he said, then I can hate him, too."

Bethany shook her head forcefully, then changed her mind and wildly shook her hand in front of her friend a couple of times. "The raise..."

"Yes?"

"The lunch..."

"Yes," Sally said, and took a step forward. "Go on."

"They weren't because Joshua is interested in me. He wants a b-a-b-y-s-i-t-t-e-r."

"What?" Sally exploded.

"He was buttering me up so I'd be his weekend baby-sitter for Angie."

Sally's eyes narrowed, and she plopped herself down on the davenport and crossed her long legs, looking more furious by the moment.

Bethany reached for a tissue and blew her nose. "I should have known he'd never be interested in a woman with small breasts," she bellowed, burying her face in the tissue.

A loyal friend, Sally sat at her side and gently patted Bethany's back. "You're not standing still for this," her roommate announced with grim determination. "I won't let you."

"Just what do 'I' plan to do?"

Sally tapped her finger over her closed lips as she mused things over. "*You're* going to find yourself a man, a real man, someone who will give J. D. Norris an inferiority complex."

"And just where am I supposed to meet this fictitious male?"

Sally's gaze narrowed all the more. "I think you already have. In fact, we've both met him."

"Oh, sure," Bethany muttered. If Sally had met someone so fabulous, then she would want him for herself. "What makes you think Joshua Norris would care if I dated a hundred men?"

"He'll care," Sally said, nodding her head. "Trust me, by the time you're through with him, he'll care."

"Bethany, look," Angie cried, pointing toward the flambeaux carriers that lined both sides of the wide cobblestone street. A golden arch of flame shot from one torch to the other. In the background, a blast of music from a jazz saxophone pierced the night, followed by the unmistakable sounds of a Dixieland band.

"This is the most exciting night of my life," Angie shouted, and dramatically placed her hand over her heart.

Even the blue funk that Bethany had been in since her luncheon date with Joshua had evaporated under the excitement of New Orleans during Mardi Gras.

"I've never seen so many people in my life," Angie shouted to be heard above the heavy noise of the milling crowd. "How's Dad ever going to find us?"

"Don't worry," Bethany answered, her voice equally loud.

"Do you think he'll like my costume?"

Bethany nodded. "He'll love it." She paused and adjusted the halo on top of the little girl's head. After hearing the story of how she'd gotten her name, Angela Catherine had insisted on dressing up like an angel, with elaborate feather wings and a golden halo. Bethany's own masquerade was far less eloquent. She'd rented an antebellum-style gown, intent on playing the role of Scarlett O'Hara. She was going to flirt and flitter and play the part of a vamp and a tease. Not in front of Angie, of course; this would all be accomplished much later for Joshua's benefit. That was, if she could find the courage to do it.

Just thinking about Sally's plan to make him jealous was enough to cause Bethany to peel open the fancy lace fan and cool her flushed face.

"Oh, look," Angie cried next, pointing toward the street once more. "There's a man on stilts."

"I certainly hope those are stilts," Bethany answered with a soft laugh. "He must be all of eight feet tall." She checked the pendant watch pinned to the bodice of her gown and reached for Angie's hand. It was time to leave their position on the sidewalk if they were going to meet Joshua on time. "We'd better start working our way toward the restaurant."

"But the parade isn't over."

"It won't be for hours yet, but I don't want to keep your father waiting."

"Okay," Angie agreed, although reluctantly.

"We'll still be able to see most of it." Bethany wasn't eager to leave, either. There was so much to see and do. Excitement arced like static electricity through the air. People were singing and dancing in the streets. Strangers were hugging and kissing one another. Laughter echoed all the way from the French Quarter to the exclusive Garden District.

Tightly gripping Angie's hand so not to lose the little girl, Bethany wove her way through the milling mass of humanity.

"Bethany, Bethany, stop," Angie shouted, her young voice filled with panic. "I lost my halo."

By the time Bethany turned around to investigate, the headpiece was gone.

"Oh, dear." There was nothing Bethany could do. The halo had apparently come loose and had been quickly carted off by a masquerader who had considered the golden circle fair game.

"Now I can't be an angel," Angie said, looking as if she were ready to resort to tears if something wasn't done quickly.

"I'm sure this happens all the time," Bethany said, thinking on her feet. "Most real angels must have a difficult time holding on to their halos, too, don't you think? I know I would."

"What happens then?"

"Then they're considered almost angels, and they have to work hard to regain their status as full angels."

"Oh, I don't mind that because it must be difficult to be perfect all the time."

"Then we'll consider Angie Norris to be almost an angel."

"Right," Angie answered, somewhat appeased.

Bethany couldn't remember ever being in a larger crowd in her life. Making progress down the people-filled streets was laborious and difficult, and the restaurant wasn't even within sight.

"Look, Bethany, there's Prince Charming."

Bethany looked up in time to see a tall handsome male astride a huge white stallion trotting down the side of Bourbon Street.

"He's stopping," Angie cried, her voice shrill with excitement.

Just as Angie claimed, the handsome prince pulled back on the reins of the powerful stallion and came to a halt in the street beside them. Bethany watched in amazed wonder as the man gave the beast over to a stranger, jumped down into the crowd and worked his way through the throng of partygoers until he stood in front of Bethany and Angie.

"Madam," he said softly, "your loveliness has captured my heart."

He wore a mask so Bethany couldn't see the upper half of his face, but she would have recognized that mouth anywhere. Joshua. It had to be Joshua Norris. It looked like him. But Joshua was tied up in a conference and wouldn't be meeting them for another half hour. It couldn't possibly be him. In addition, he would never do anything this wildly romantic.

"Oh, Bethany, he's so handsome. Don't you think so?"

The prince laid out his palm, silently requesting her hand. By this time, several people had formed a circle and gathered around them, watching the unfolding scene.

"Are you going to stand there all night or are you going to kiss her?" a gruff male voice shouted.

"If he wants a kiss, I'm willing," a boisterous female voice added, and the crowd laughed.

Clearly trying to appease the fickle group of merrymakers, the handsome prince took Bethany in his arms, swung her around with a flair that drew a round of applause and draped her over his forearm. Bethany's eyes went as round as satellite dishes when he lowered his mouth to claim hers. She had half a mind to object. After all, she wasn't in the habit of kissing strange men. But this was Mardi Gras, a special once-a-year time to let down one's hair and participate in the unconventional.

The prince's mouth took hers in a warm moist kiss that was as soul stirring as a religious revival and as deep as a bottomless sea. The kiss gentled as the fierce hunger was satisfied, and his lips moved over hers like the gentle brush of a spring sun on a hungry earth.

The crowd approved heartily.

When the prince released Bethany it was a wonder she didn't melt onto the sidewalk. Breathless and weak, she placed her hand over her heart, heedless to anything but the man who had held her in his arms. She blinked and took a step back.

"Wow," Angie said, her eyes round and wide. "I thought he was going to suck your lips off."

Had Bethany been any less affected, she might have laughed, but even breathing was difficult . . . laughing would have been impossible.

Three or four women formed an impromptu line. "We've got dibs next," the first one called out, waving her fingers.

The prince, clearly being a true gentleman, kissed the hand of each woman in turn and, before they could object, gracefully remounted his white stallion and rode off.

"Bethany, why did he kiss you?" Angie wanted to know.

"I . . . I don't know." She continued to watch him long after he rode out of sight. "Angie—" she paused and looked down at the ten-year-old "—did that man . . . the one who kissed me . . . did he remind you of anyone?"

"Oh, yes," Angie admitted. "He looked like the guy in Cinderella. The one who kept trying the glass slipper on all the women's feet. I always thought that was a little silly, you know. What woman buys glass shoes these days?"

"Oh." Bethany couldn't help being disappointed. It was nonsensical to think it could have been Joshua when it simply wasn't possible. The logistics were all wrong.

And yet . . .

Chapter Six

The noise level decreased by several decibels when Bethany and Angie left the street and entered the restaurant where they were supposed to meet Joshua. Antoine's was probably the most famous restaurant in New Orleans, having been in operation close to 150 years. Bethany secretly hoped her employer wouldn't be there. If the prince who'd kissed her *had* been Joshua, then it would have been close to impossible for him to have changed outfits so quickly and gotten to Antoine's before them.

Her gaze searched the plush interior, and to Bethany's bitter disappointment, she found Joshua casually sitting at a table awaiting their arrival.

"Dad, Dad, guess what I saw!" Angie went running past the maître d', weaving her way between tables to her father, then hurling her arms around his neck and squeezing for all she was worth.

The maître d' offered Bethany a strained smile and formally escorted her to Joshua's table. He paused and elegantly held out a shield-back chair for her to take a seat.

"There was a man eight feet tall," Angie was telling Joshua, the words running together she was speaking so fast. "And other men who tossed fire at each other and then, oh, then we met a handsome prince on a big white horse who kissed Bethany. It was so-o romantic."

Joshua's eyes widened, and when he glanced toward his secretary, the edges of his mouth were quivering with the effort to hold back a smile. "It sounds like you've had quite an evening."

"Oh, yes, and, Dad, there are so many people here, and everyone dresses like it's Halloween." Angie paused and her hand flew to her hair. "I lost my halo. I was going to surprise you by being an angel because you said I looked like one, and then I lost the most important part, but Bethany said it was all right because I could be almost an angel and that's really better, because angels are supposed to be perfect, and well, you know me."

"I do indeed know you." Joshua looked up and grinned in Bethany's direction. "I'm pleased to see you made it safely."

She managed a nod, still watching him closely, hoping to prove, if only to herself, that the prince who kissed her had been Joshua. She so desperately wanted it to be him and would always choose to believe that it had been.

"Do you usually kiss strange men on the street, Miss Stone?" he asked, seeming to read her thoughts.

"I . . . I . . ." she stammered. She couldn't very well announce that she thought the man had been him, had dreamed it was Joshua, and that was the only reason she'd allowed the prince to take her in his arms.

"It wasn't like Bethany had much choice, Dad," Angie inserted, climbing off her father's lap and taking her own seat.

"So the brute forced you?"

Bethany kept her gaze lowered to her lap while she smoothed a linen napkin over the top of her thighs. "Not exactly."

Joshua leaned forward, rested his elbows on the table and clasped his fingers together. "I'm curious why you would allow a complete stranger to sweep you into his arms and kiss you in front of an onlooking crowd."

Hope fired through Bethany's blood like running water shooting off the edge of a cliff. It had been Joshua! It must have been, because no one had told him about the prince taking her in his arms or that a crowd had gathered around and had been watching.

Boldly she raised her gaze to his. "He didn't seem the least bit dangerous," she said softly. "I . . . I felt that I knew him."

Joshua cocked his thick eyebrows. "I see."

Bethany certainly hoped he did because her heart was pounding like a crazed pogo stick.

"Dad, is Bethany coming over Friday night?" Angie asked, sticking her head around the side of the huge oblong menu. "You said she was."

"Bethany?" Joshua fielded the question to her. From the way he studied the menu it appeared that her answer was of little consequence to him.

This piece of news frustrated Bethany. Joshua hadn't said anything to her about needing her Friday night. He'd taken for granted that she didn't have any other plans, which fortunately she didn't, but his blatant assumption irked her.

"I suppose I could be there Friday night," she mumbled somewhat ungraciously.

"Mrs. Larson would be more than willing to stay," Joshua announced in a flat emotionless voice. "There's no need to feel obligated, especially if you have other plans."

"I'm not doing anything special." Bethany's admission took some of the bite out of her irritation.

"Oh, good," Angie said with an elaborate sigh. "Weekends are a dead bore, and being with Bethany is always such fun."

"Have you thought about inviting a school friend to spend the night?" Bethany asked. "We could order pizza and rent movies."

Angie slammed the menu down on top of the table, her eyes round and excited. "We could do all that?"

"Mr. Norris . . . Joshua?" It gave Bethany a small amount of pleasure to toss the question back into his court.

"Pizza and rented movies and a friend for the night?" He didn't sound overly enthused by any of Bethany's suggestions. "I suppose that won't be any problem."

"I think I'll ask Melissa over," Angie murmured thoughtfully, nibbling on her lower lip. "No, I like Wendy Miller better. She wants to be a writer, like me, and when we get tired of watching videos, we could make up our own stories."

"That sounds like an excellent plan," Bethany said, pleased. "Don't you think so, Joshua?"

He mumbled something under his breath about pizza and little girls running around the house at six in the morning and left it at that.

The remainder of the week passed quickly. What Joshua had said about the next few months being especially busy for him and the company was true. Rarely could Bethany remember a time when Joshua had more meetings and appointments scheduled. He was working too hard and it showed. Bethany wished there was some way she could lessen his load.

"Do you have the Harrison report typed for me yet?" he asked Thursday at quitting time.

"Not yet," Bethany admitted reluctantly, feeling guilty. The report was nearly two hundred pages in length and highly complicated. "I can stay late tonight if you want."

"No." He shook his head. "But give it top priority first thing in the morning."

"Of course. I apologize, Joshua, but there were a thousand interruptions the past couple of days." She felt obliged to explain why it was taking so long, although he didn't appear to be upset with her.

"Don't worry about it, Bethany, I understand."

Friday, Bethany skipped her lunch hour to work on the report so Joshua would have it for his meeting that evening. It was on his desk when he returned late that afternoon.

He called her into his office soon afterward and motioned for her to sit down.

"You did an excellent job with this," he told her, granting her a rare office-hour smile.

"Thank you." She was rather proud of it herself.

Joshua hesitated and leaned back in his chair, looking anxious. "The dinner meeting is with a group of financiers this evening. I don't know what time I'll be getting back to the house. I'm afraid it could be quite late."

"Don't worry. I can stay with Angie and her friend until you're home."

"I really appreciate your help, Bethany."

She nodded, unable to voice the emotion that ran like a river deep within her heart. Helping Joshua, sharing his joys and dividing his worries was something she yearned to do every day. Since Angie's arrival their relationship had changed drastically, and yet she wanted so much more.

It was after eleven by the time Bethany heard Joshua let himself into the house. She'd been sitting in the family room reading. Both Angie and Wendy had fallen asleep at ten, exhausted from a busy school week. The pair of preteens were sleeping in Angie's bedroom and the house had been joyfully quiet.

Bethany set her book aside and stood, eager to talk to Joshua about this important meeting. She knew that the future of Norris Pharmaceutical rested on the decision of the financiers, although Joshua had never directly told her as much. She would have had to be blind not to have known the problems his company was currently facing.

Bethany met Joshua in the living room and greeted him with a warm smile. "Welcome home," she said softly, not wanting to wake the girls.

"It's good to be here." He set his briefcase down, peeled off his suit jacket and folded it over the top of the sofa. "How did everything go?"

"Great, what about you?"

Joshua shrugged. "I won't know their decision until next week sometime."

So Joshua and Norris Pharmaceutical were going to be forced to play a waiting game.

"Are you hungry?" Bethany asked.

Joshua nodded, looking slightly chagrined. "Starved, as a matter of fact. I didn't have much of an appetite earlier."

Understanding the importance of this meeting, Bethany could well believe that. She'd eaten sparingly herself. "There's plenty of pizza left."

"You'll join me?" he asked. When she nodded, he looked pleased and led the way into the kitchen. "I think I've got a couple of cold beers. Do you want one?"

"Please."

While Joshua was searching through the refrigerator for the bottles of beer, Bethany placed several slices of cold pizza on a plate and warmed them in the microwave. By the time they were heated, Joshua had brought down paper napkins and set those and the two bottles of beer on the small kitchen table.

The pepperoni pizza was excellent, better than the first time around, she decided. They didn't talk much at first. Joshua asked her a couple of questions about how her evening had gone with Angie and her bosom buddy, Wendy, and she told him how the two had been far too keen to make up their own stories to be interested in watching the movie Bethany had rented.

"Since they didn't view it earlier, I've set up the television and VCR so all Angie has to do is turn them on first thing in the morning. Hopefully that'll give you an extra hour or two of peace so you can sleep in a little." She worried that Joshua wasn't getting enough rest. Lord knew he worked long enough hours, especially lately.

"That was thoughtful of you."

A short silence followed before Joshua spoke again. It was clear that the gathering with the financiers continued to weigh on his mind. He told her his general feelings about how the reception to his proposal had gone, the vibes he'd felt, the mood that had persisted throughout the long dinner meeting.

Bethany leaned back and listened attentively while he rummaged through and sorted out his thoughts. He finished, sat quietly for a moment, then downed the last of his beer.

"I suppose I should be getting home," Bethany said, standing.

Joshua's gaze flew to his gold watch. He looked surprised when he noted the time. "I didn't mean to keep you so long, Beth."

She stopped in front of the dishwasher, turned back to him and smiled.

"Does something amuse you?"

She opened the kitchen appliance and set their dirty plates inside. "There was a time not so long ago when you didn't know my first name."

"I knew," he whispered. He was so close behind her that she could feel his warm breath against the side of her neck. "I've always known."

A shiver of awareness scooted down Bethany's spine and she braced her hands against the counter as Joshua gently cupped her shoulders, his touch so light that she thought, at first, she might have imagined it. His fingers gently stroked her skin as he ran his hands down the length of her arms. At the same time, he tenderly drew her back so her body fit against his full height. His movements were slow, deliberate, as though he expected her to object and were granting her ample opportunity to pull away if she wanted.

Bethany went completely immobile. She couldn't have moved had her life depended on it.

Joshua rested his chin on top of her head for a short moment before he paused and lowered his mouth to the slender curve of her neck. The instant his lips touched her sensitized skin and located the pulsing vein there, heat erupted like a fiery volcano throughout Bethany's trembling body.

She didn't know who moved first. She might have initiated the action by turning and slipping her arms around his waist, or Joshua's hands could have directed her. Bethany didn't know which. It didn't matter, though, nothing did except that she was in

Joshua's arms and his mouth was hungrily locked over hers. He was kissing her as if he'd thought of doing nothing else for endless hours. Again and again he dragged his lips over hers, as though the thought of releasing her so soon were too much to bear.

A helpless moan escaped Bethany. To have Joshua kiss her was almost like drowning, she thought, then bursting through the water's clear surface and feeling more alive than at any other time in her life.

Still holding her, Joshua buried his face in the curve of her neck and exhaled a deep unsteady breath.

"The most important meeting of my life," he whispered, his voice husky and moist against her flushed skin. "And all I could think about was you."

"Oh, Joshua." She tucked her hands under his arms and leaned against him for support, bracing her forehead against his hard chest.

"This shouldn't be happening," he complained, but there was no regret in his voice.

"I wanted it, too," she admitted. "Joshua," she whispered, hiding her face in his chest and closing her eyes to the warm happy feeling that enveloped her.

"You've been so good for Angie," he whispered.

Some of the good feelings left Bethany and she stiffened, fearing he was going to use her love for him to keep her as a willing baby-sitter. "I see," she whispered in a soft broken voice.

Her hold relaxed and she tried to break away, but Joshua wouldn't let her. "What's wrong?" he asked anxiously. "Bethany, you've gone all cold on me. What did I say?"

"Nothing."

"You're angry because I appreciate what a good friend you are to my daughter?"

He lovingly caressed the side of her jaw and lifted her chin so that she couldn't avoid meeting his gaze. "No, of course not. I love Angie."

"And she loves you." He bent forward and brushed his mouth over hers, his lips settling naturally onto hers for another swift sample.

She kept her eyes closed, still trapped in the lingering sensation, and yet her heart felt as if it were weighted down with bricks. It wasn't right that she should be in his arms and feel so terribly insecure. Joshua should know her feelings. "I sometimes think Angie's the only reason you...you want to be around me."

The room went suspiciously quiet. The smallest noise would have sounded like a sonic boom in the silence that stretched between them. Bethany's eyes fluttered open, but she dared not look at Joshua, dared not meet the fiery anger she could feel radiating from him.

"You don't honestly believe that, do you?"

"What else am I to think?"

He freed her arms and took a step back from her. His eyes were dark and solemn. Sad. "If you don't know the answer to that by now, then I've failed us both."

"Failed us both?" She tossed his own words back at him. "The only time you ever want me around is to...to baby-sit for Angie."

The muscles in his jaw leaped with the effort to control his anger. "I can't see where you'd ever think that."

Bethany felt miserable. Only a minute before he'd been holding and kissing her and now he looked as though he couldn't wait for her to get out of his home.

Trembling from the inside out, she returned to the kitchen table and removed their crumpled napkins.

"Leave those," he barked.

"I . . . I was just going to put them in the garbage."

"I don't want to be accused of using you as my personal maid sometime later. Believe me, I'd prefer to do the task myself."

If he'd struck her, he couldn't have hurt Bethany any more. Tears bled out of her eyes and she jerked her head away, not wanting him to know how sensitive she was to his cruel barbs. The words to tell him she was leaving didn't make it past the tight constriction in her throat. The only thing left for her to do was walk away. She collected her purse and her book and was almost to the front door when Joshua reached out and stopped her.

Still she didn't turn to look back at him.

"Beth," he said starkly. "I'm sorry."

Her head whirled around and she saw the regret written boldly across his face.

"I'm sorry, too, Joshua." Sorry to have doubted him, sorry to have been so willing to believe the worst of him, but she couldn't help it. She may have done him a grave injustice . . . but she doubted it.

He kissed her again, but this one lacked the urgency or the hunger of the others. With his arm

wrapped around her waist, he walked her out to her
car. As she drove away, Bethany could see Joshua's
image in her rearview mirror, standing alone in the
night, watching her long after she pulled away.

"Okay, everything's all set," Sally announced,
standing in front of Bethany's desk. She wore that off-
center silly smile that told Bethany her roommate was
up to something.

Bethany paused with her fingers poised over the
typewriter keyboard. She would play along with Sally's game for a while, until she recognized what card
Sally was hiding up her sleeve, but that wouldn't take
too long. "What's all set?" she asked.

"Your hot date."

"What?" Bethany exploded, and jerked her gaze
toward the connecting door, grateful it was closed so
Joshua wouldn't overhear their conversation. "A hot
date with who?"

"Whom," her roommate corrected with a mischie-
vous grin.

"Whom, then!"

"You honestly don't remember, do you?" Sally
looked surprised, then stunned, then impatient.
Watching each emotion was like viewing the flickering movements of an old-time silent film. "You really
don't!"

"Obviously not," Bethany answered. "What are
you talking about?"

With a look of disgusted dismay, Sally crossed her
arms and aimed her chin toward the ceiling fixture.
"Does the name Jerry Johnson ring a bell?"

Bethany mulled it over in her mind. She knew Sally had been up to something the past couple of days, but she hadn't a clue what. "I find the name vaguely familiar."

"Well, you *should*, since you've agreed to a date with him."

"I've what?" This nightmare was growing more vivid by the minute. "When?" Bethany demanded.

"I've arranged everything for Thursday night."

"Not that when," Bethany bellowed. "When did I ever say I'd have anything to do with the man?"

Sally cast a suspicious glance toward Joshua's door. "The afternoon you sat in our living room going through tissues like they were chocolate bunnies at Easter. We made plans, you and I."

The image jarred Bethany's memory. She could remember her friend telling her what a fool she was being and that she would be an ever bigger one if she continued to let Joshua Norris take advantage of her. Sally had prattled on about finding a man to make Joshua jealous, but Bethany had been too miserable to listen carefully. Now she realized her mistake.

"I seem to remember you making a suggestion or two," Bethany admitted reluctantly.

"I did more than suggest," Sally said righteously, and lowered her voice to a hissing whisper. "I *acted*, which is more than I can say for you."

"But everything is progressing nicely between me and Joshua," Bethany answered in like tones, keeping her voice as low as possible. "I don't want to do anything to topple the cart."

"Sure, it's going just wonderful between you and the great white hunter," Sally scoffed. "You're taking care of his little girl every free moment. You don't have time for anything else."

"But..."

"Just answer me one thing, Beth. Has your precious Mr. J. D. Norris ever taken *you* out without dragging Angie along? Has it ever been just the two of you alone? Well?"

Her roommate knocked away Bethany's argument as easily as if she'd toppled a stack of children's building blocks. Bethany lowered her gaze, feeling miserable and lost. Even their one luncheon date alone had been an excuse to get her to watch Angie.

"See what I mean?" Sally muttered. "Mr. Norris is using you. He has been from the first, and as your best friend I refuse to stand by and let it happen. You've got to start circulating again. I'm going to introduce you to the *right* kind of men, and I won't let you stop me."

"But, Sally..."

"I refuse to hear any more arguments. Thursday night, understand."

"All right," Bethany agreed, but she couldn't have cared less about Jerry Johnson or Jerry anyone. She was in love with Joshua, and nothing would change the way she felt about her employer.

When Joshua called for her to take some dictation an hour later, Bethany briskly stepped into his office.

He smiled when he saw her, but her returning smile was strained.

"Is the Hanson report finished yet?" he asked.

"Almost, I'll have it on your desk in a few minutes."

"Good." He handed her a stack of papers. "Collate and get me fifteen copies of each of these at your convenience. There isn't any big rush."

"Is tomorrow morning soon enough?"

"That'll be fine."

Bethany would have returned to the reception area, but Joshua stopped her. "One minute, Miss Stone." He paused to write across the top of a yellow legal tablet, and when he glanced up, he looked pleased about something, relaxed in a way she hadn't ever seen in him. "Would you happen to be free tomorrow night, Beth?"

Bethany felt as if a loaded logging truck had parked on top of her chest. "Thursday night?"

"That's tomorrow. I realize it's short notice. Is there a problem?"

Her palms felt unexpectedly moist and she hoisted the papers she was holding to get a better grip on them. The small stack felt as though it weighed thirty pounds. "I'm sorry, Joshua...Mr. Norris, but I've already got plans."

"There's no problem. I should have asked you earlier." He frowned and went back to his task, scratching notes across the top of the pad.

"If...I'm sure Mrs. Larson will be able to stay with Angie, but if she can't—"

"Mrs. Larson can, so don't worry about it."

Bethany was trembling by the time she made it to her desk. Her knees were actually knocking against each other when she sat down. She could feel her heart's thundering beat all the way to her toes.

"Bethany..." Sally stuck her head around the door. "Have you got a moment?"

"Sally!" She groaned. "What is it now?"

Her friend strolled into the office. "I've got his picture."

"Whose?"

"Jerry Johnson's." She looked as pleased as if she'd managed to smuggle secret papers out of the Kremlin. "It was in the bottom of my purse. I forgot I had it."

"Sally, honestly, I don't even want to go out with this guy."

"Don't say that until you've seen his picture." She waved the photograph under Bethany's nose, as though the blurred image would be enough to convince her how lucky she was to be dating such a hunk.

Bethany grabbed the small glossy picture from her friend's hands and studied the handsome smiling face. Jerry Johnson was attractive—okay, he was downright showstopping.

Sally leaned her hip against the side of Bethany's desk, crossed her arms and looked exceedingly proud of herself. "He knows you, too."

"Why don't I remember him?" She frowned because he *did* look vaguely familiar.

"You only met him once," Sally said, and studied the length of her fingernails on her right hand. "Christmas, last year, at the Dawsons' party."

Bethany could hardly remember who the Dawsons were until she recalled they were family friends of Sally's.

"Trust me, Beth. Thursday night with Jerry Johnson is a date you won't soon forget."

"Ms. Livingston," Joshua said in a cold hard voice from the open doorway. "Seeing that you have nothing to do but traipse in and out of my office at all times of the day, I'm wondering just how much your work efforts contribute to my company."

Sally bounced away from the desk as though she'd been sitting on a hot plate. Her eyes filled with shock as she glanced to Bethany, silently pleading for help.

"Sally was making a delivery," Bethany said, stretching the truth as far as she dare.

"Yes, I heard. The photo of your hot date."

Bethany's face flushed with brilliant color.

"I trust you two have more important business to see to on company time?"

"Yes, sir," Sally mumbled, and was gone.

"Are those papers copied for me yet?" Joshua demanded of Bethany.

"I . . . no. I'll take care of that first thing in the morning."

"I need them now."

"But you said—"

"Don't argue with me, Miss Stone. I want those papers copied and collated before you leave tonight. Is that clear?"

"Perfectly, Mr. Norris."

"Good. And the next time I see Ms. Livingston in my office talking to you on company time instead of

being where she should be, she'll be looking for another job.''

"If Sally leaves, then I'm going, as well.''

"That decision is your own, Miss Stone.'' With that
he spun around and returned to his office, soundly
closing the door.

Chapter Seven

Have aliens captured your brain?'' Bethany demanded of her roommate. ''Of all the crazy things you've pulled over the years, I—''

''I know...I know,'' Sally cut her off, still pale from her brief confrontation with J. D. Norris. Her hands went to her throat. ''Honestly, I thought he was going to ask for my head.''

''He damn near did.'' She didn't mention that hers would have rolled with her friend's. Joshua had been in such an ill temper that even hours after their confrontation, talking to him would have been impossible. Not that Bethany had tried. She knew her employer well enough to recognize his mood. And honor it.

''You're still going Thursday night, aren't you?'' Sally asked, glancing surreptitiously toward her good friend.

"Of course I'm going." But Bethany didn't feel nearly as confident as she sounded. This whole idea of dating a man she'd briefly met at a Christmas party months earlier didn't suit her, especially since she'd been drinking eggnog at the time. Eggnog and wine were synonymous with trouble as far as Bethany was concerned.

Friday morning, Joshua was already at his desk when Bethany arrived. She paused between the doorway that connected their two offices, surprised to see him and dismayed at the sight he made. Joshua looked terrible. Even from where she was standing, Bethany could see and feel his fatigue. Dark smudges circled his eyes. His jacket had long since been discarded, his tie loosened and the top two buttons of his wrinkled shirt unfastened. One glance convinced Bethany he hadn't bothered to go home the night before.

"Joshua," she whispered, the concern chugging through her blood, "how long have you been here?"

Deliberately he set his pencil aside but continued to hold on to it. "When we're at the office, Miss Stone, kindly refer to me as Mr. Norris."

"As you wish," she returned stiffly, and proceeded into the room. So that was the way it was to be. Fine. Holding her back as rigid as possible, she put on a fresh pot of coffee and went back to her own desk to sort through the morning mail. When she'd finished, she returned, poured Joshua a cup of coffee and delivered it to him the way she had every morning for the past three years.

"So, Miss Stone," he said sardonically, "how did your 'hot date' go?"

His voice was so thick with sarcasm that Bethany had to bite down on her bottom lip to keep from responding in like tones.

"Fine, thank you." She handed him the sorted mail. "The letter you've been looking for from Charles Youngblood arrived."

"Good." Joshua picked through the stack until he located it. "Are you planning on seeing him again?" he demanded.

"Charles Youngblood?"

"You're being deliberately obtuse. I was referring to your... date," he said with a sneer.

"I hardly think that's any of your business," she snapped, her own patience a slender thread. "What happens outside this office isn't your concern."

"When your action directly affects the productivity of this company, I'd damn well say it's my business."

Icy fingers wrapped themselves around Bethany's vocal chords. She couldn't have answered Joshua had her job depended on it, and considering the horrible mood he was in, it very well could be.

"Miss Stone, I asked you a question. I expect an answer."

It was in her mind to shout he was a monster and that she refused to discuss details of her dates with any employer. Instead, she squarely met his gaze and said, "My personal life is my own." Following that, she turned and walked out of the office.

An hour later, her hands were still trembling, and she remained on the verge of tears. The door to Joshua's office opened and just the sound was enough to cause Bethany to stiffen her spine, readying herself for another confrontation.

He walked over to her desk and set down the mail. A list of handwritten instructions accompanied the large stack of letters.

"Cancel my appointments for the day, Miss Stone," he said in a raspy whisper.

Bethany refused to look at him, but with her peripheral vision she saw him lean momentarily against the edge of her desk and pinch the bridge of his nose. He paused and wiped his hand down his face.

"I'm going home," he announced.

She nodded her head in quick jerky movements.

Joshua hesitated once more. "I apologize for my earlier behavior. You're absolutely right—your personal life is your own. I had no business flying into you that way."

Again she remained silent.

"If there's anything that requires my attention, you can contact me at the house. Good day, Miss Stone."

"Mr. Norris."

"J. D. Norris said all that," Sally murmured, her eyes narrowed and thoughtful.

"I've never seen him so angry and unreasonable. I'm just glad he left because I couldn't have stood another minute... I think I would have quit on the spot if he'd said one more thing."

Sally broke off a part of her sugar-coated doughnut and poised it in front of her mouth. "I think he could be falling in love with you, Beth."

The sip of coffee Bethany had just swallowed jammed halfway down her throat and refused to budge. She slapped her hand over her chest and gasped. Once she'd composed herself enough to speak, she murmured, "Oh, hardly."

"I mean it," Sally countered with that thoughtful contemplative look of hers. "He's acting like a jealous little boy, which is exactly what I thought might happen. The extent of his reaction confirms my suspicions."

"A more likely scenario is that I was a convenient scapegoat for him to vent his troubles." Bethany wasn't blind to the financial problems in which Norris Pharmaceutical was currently involved. Having recently held off one takeover effort, Joshua had been hit almost immediately by another. His resources had been depleted by the first attempt and he was holding on to the control of the company by the thinnest of threads. Naturally, most of the information had been privileged, and she wasn't at liberty to discuss it with anyone, including her best friend. A good deal of what transpired had been between Joshua and other business leaders without Bethany being present. But she'd garnered enough information of what was going on from the numerous transcripts she'd typed. Unfortunately, she didn't have a clue how Joshua was surviving this latest takeover bid.

"I don't know," Sally muttered with the same piece of doughnut still level with her lips. "I've been doing a lot of thinking about the way Mr. Norris has been acting these past few weeks, and it's obvious he's enthralled with you."

"Sure he is," Bethany muttered scornfully. "Angie thinks I'm great fun and Joshua Norris knows I'm a soft touch when it comes to his daughter."

"Well, aren't you?"

Bethany was reluctantly forced to agree. "I...won't be able to meet you at Charley's after work," she informed her friend, almost as an afterthought.

"How come?"

"I . . . I've got to take some papers over to Mr. Norris's house for him to sign."

"Ah." Sally's eyes brightened, then were quickly lowered as she pretended an interest in her paper napkin. "Listen..." She paused, placed the half-eaten doughnut back on her plate and brushed the sugar granules from her fingertips. "Since you weren't really all that interested in Jerry Johnson, I was wondering..."

"Go ahead," Bethany said, having trouble disguising a smile, almost enjoying her friend's discomfort. "Go ahead and what?"

"Date Jerry yourself. Do you honestly think I didn't know you're crazy about him? Sally, you drool every time someone mentions his name."

"I do?"

"Either that, or your eyes start to water. I can't believe you'd fix *me* up with a date with him when you're so obviously taken with him yourself." Actually, knowing Sally's twisted way of planning things, this scheme of hers was probably the only way she could come up with to talk to him again.

"You knew?" Sally demanded.

"Not at first," Bethany was slow to admit. She'd been so caught up with what was going on between her and Joshua that she hadn't been paying attention to her friend until the obvious practically hit her over the head. After all, how many women carried a picture of a man they'd only met once, in their purse for an entire year? Not many, she would bet. Only someone as sentimental and romantic as Sally.

"So you don't mind if I—"

"Not in the least. Jerry Johnson is all yours, with my blessing."

Bethany finished the last of her duties at five and left the office to drive directly to Joshua's home on Lake Pontchartrain. Her excuse to stop at the house was flimsy at best, but she felt terrible about what had happened that morning and longed to straighten things out—even if it meant admitting she wouldn't be seeing Jerry again.

Mrs. Larson opened the front door. "Miss Stone, how are you this afternoon?"

The portly widow with thick silver hair wore a black uniform and a large white apron. She was kind and gentle-hearted, and on the few occasions that Bethany had met her, she'd been impressed with the older woman.

"I'm fine, thank you," Bethany answered. "How's Mr. Norris?"

Mrs. Larson's lips thinned with worry as she shook her head. "I swear it's a miracle that man hasn't worked himself into an early grave."

"I know," Bethany said miserably. "Has he slept at all?" The more she thought about their argument that morning, the more guilty she felt for her part in it. Joshua was obviously exhausted beyond reason.

"He slept an hour or two early this morning, and then he was at his desk in the den, working. Would you like me to take you to him?"

"Please." Bethany followed Mrs. Larson to the large den, which was built off the living room and faced the lake.

The older woman knocked politely, then opened the door. "Miss Stone is here to see you," she announced, and stepped aside.

Joshua half rose from his sitting position. "Bethany." His eyes widened with surprise. "Were there problems? You should have phoned."

"I apologize for interrupting you . . ."

"It's no problem. Sit down."

She lowered herself into a huge overstuffed leather chair and folded her hands on her lap, watching him expectantly. If she didn't know better, she would have sworn he was pleased to see her, and that made her feel good about her unscheduled visit.

He returned her look, his gaze expectant, and she suddenly remembered the excuse she'd invented to come to the house. "There are some letters for you to sign... I seem to have left them in the car." She rushed to her feet. "I'll get them and be right back."

She was such an idiot! Bethany all but jumped out of the chair and hurried back outside. Instead of troubling Mrs. Larson a second time, she let herself into the house and Joshua's den.

"Taking the time to bring these over was thoughtful," he said, scribbling his name across the bottom of the first letter without bothering to read it.

"Yes... well, I felt badly about this morning," she murmured. Her face was growing warm and she knew she was blushing. "You'd obviously been up all night and, although it really wasn't any of your concern, it wouldn't have hurt me any to let you know about Jerry and me.''

"Yes?'' he coaxed when she didn't immediately continue. "So you've decided to continue dating Ms. Livingston's friend?'' Some of the pleasure drained from his eyes. "Well, that's understandable.''

"No, Joshua... I mean, Mr. Norris. I won't be seeing Jerry again.''

"You won't?'' Five years were peeled off his face as his expression lightened considerably. "Well, that's certainly your business.''

"Yes, I know,'' she countered softly. With no excuse to linger any longer, Bethany stood, wishing she could find a plausible reason to stay. "How's Angie?'' she asked with a flash of brilliance, and reclaimed her chair.

"She's doing just fine,'' Joshua answered eagerly. "Good. She's spending the night with her friend Wendy.''

Silence followed.

Bethany stood once more.

"She seems to have made the adjustment from New York to New Orleans rather well.''

Bethany sat back down, almost gleeful with relief to stay. "Yes, I thought so.''

Another moment of silence fell between them.

"I know this is spur-of-the-moment, but would you care to have dinner with me?'' Joshua asked.

"Yes.'' Bethany felt excited enough about the prospect to stand up and do cheers, and she had to restrain herself. "I'd like that a lot.''

The smile he tossed her was almost boyish. He paused and glanced her way, eyeing her clothes, and frowned slightly.

"I can go home and change if you want." She was wearing a dark blue business suit with a straight skirt and short double-breasted jacket.

"No, you're perfect just the way you are."

"You're sure?" She was curious to know where he was taking her. When he'd asked her to dinner, she'd assumed at first that he meant for her to eat with him here at the house.

"I'm positive," he answered, although he was dressed far more casually than usual himself, in slacks and a thick Irish cable-knit sweater the color of winter wheat.

After pausing to let Mrs. Larson know he was leaving, Joshua reached for Bethany's hand and led her out of the house. He drove into the heart of the city and parked on a side street a few blocks off the French Quarter.

"Do you like beans and rice?" he asked.

Bethany nodded eagerly. The popular New Orleans dish had been elevated with the recent interest in Cajun and Creole cooking. The recipe had originated in the slave quarters and many a Southerner had grown up in a time when each day's menu revolved around rice and beans.

"A friend of mine operates a café that serves the best Louisiana cooking in the world." He hesitated and smiled. "But be warned, the food is fantastic, but the place rates low on atmosphere."

"You needn't worry about that with me." She wondered what he would think if he were ever to join her large family for a Sunday dinner. How would he fit in with mismatched place settings, gas-station handout water glasses and an ever-flowing stream of conversation?

Joshua slipped his arm around her waist, holding her close to his side. "I wasn't worried that you'd disapprove, I just wanted to warn you."

"Okay, I consider myself properly warned," she told him, her eyes smiling. This was the man she was just beginning to know, the man she'd been granted rare glimpses of over the years. Excitement fired through her blood.

Joshua directed her down a narrow alleyway. Bethany had been up and down the streets in the French Quarter most of her life, but she didn't recognize this one.

"Are you sure there's a restaurant back here?" she asked.

"Positive."

The place was small and cramped, with only a handful of tables. The chairs were mismatched and the Formica on the tabletops was chipped, but the smells wafting from the kitchen were enough to convince Bethany that Joshua knew what he was talking about.

"What you doin' bringing that skinny chil' in my kitchen J. D. Norris?" A huge black woman stepped out from behind an old-fashioned cash register.

"Bethany, meet Cleo."

The woman wiped her hands dry on the smudged apron that was tucked into the folds of her skirt. "You looks like a strong wind would blow you away," Cleo announced, cocking her head to one side as she studied Bethany through dark narrowed eyes.

"Then I sincerely hope you intend to feed me."

Cleo chuckled and her whole torso shook with the action. "Honey chil', you have no idea how Cleo can feed a soul." She ambled across the room and pulled back two chairs. "Sit," she ordered. With that she started toward the kitchen, paused and looked over her shoulder. "You bring your horn?"

Joshua nodded. "It's in the car."

"It's been too long, Dizzy, much too long."

"Your horn? Dizzy?" Bethany asked, once Cleo was out of sight.

"I play saxophone now and then, when the spirit moves me."

Shocked speechless, Bethany studied him for a moment, astonished at this side of this complex man that she'd never known existed. There was nothing in her experiences with Joshua that had so much as hinted at any musical interest or talent. "I had no idea," she managed to say after a moment.

He grinned, as if to say there was a lot about him she didn't know, and Bethany couldn't doubt it.

Cleo returned with plates piled high with rice and smothered with rich beans in a red sauce. "This is just for openers," Cleo warned, setting down the two plates. She returned a minute later with a third stacked high with warm squares of corn bread oozing with melted butter.

"She doesn't honestly expect us to eat all this?" Bethany asked between bites. She'd tasted beans and rice in any number of restaurants but never anything that could compare with this unusual blend of spices, vegetables and meat. Nothing had ever tasted anywhere near this delicious.

"She'd be insulted if we left a crumb."

Bethany didn't know how she managed it, but her plate was clean when Cleo returned. The black woman gave her a broad grin and nodded approvingly.

"Maybe you be all right after all," the massive woman said with a sparkle in her dark eyes.

"Maybe you be, too," Bethany returned, holding in a laugh.

The huge woman let loose with a loud burst of laughter and slapped Joshua across the back. "I like her."

Joshua grinned, sharing a look with Bethany. "So do I."

"You got room for my special sweet-potato-pecan pie?" Cleo eyed them both speculatively, as if to say these skinny white folks didn't know nothin' about good food.

Joshua leaned back, splayed his fingers over his stomach and sighed. "I think you better count me out. I'm stuffed to the gills. Bethany?"

"Bring me a piece."

Cleo nodded several times. "You done yourself proud, Dizzy. She don't look like much, but there's more to her than meets the eye."

The pie was thick, sweet and delicious.

Joshua sat back and watched, eyes wide, as Bethany finished off the last bite.

"You amaze me."

Bethany licked the ends of her fingers. "I told you before, I've got a healthy appetite."

Cleo returned, carrying two steaming mugs of coffee. "You takin' this honey chil' to St. Peter's?"

Joshua nodded, and Cleo looked pleased.

After Joshua paid for their meal, he led Bethany out of the café and further down the narrow alley to another set of doors. "I hope you like jazz because you're about to get an earful."

"I love any kind of music," Bethany was quick to tell him, feeling closer to Joshua than ever before. He opened the door off the alley and a cloud of smoke as thick as a bayou fog covered them as they walked through the door. It took Bethany a second to adjust her eyesight to the dim interior. She couldn't see much as Joshua led her to a vacant table and pulled out a chair for her. The sounds of clicking ice, the tinny tones of an old piano and the hum of conversation surrounded her like the familiar greetings of old friends.

"What would you like to drink?" Joshua asked, and had to lean close in order for Bethany to hear him above the conversational hum. "A mint julep?"

She answered him with a shake of her head. "A beer, please."

Joshua turned to leave her. He must have forgotten something because he hadn't gone more than a couple of steps when he turned back. Bethany looked up expectantly and he leaned down to press his mouth over hers in a kiss so fleeting Bethany had no time to describe it even to herself.

In the front of the room was a small platform stage. A man was playing the piano and another was setting up a drum set. Bethany watched Joshua weave a path between tables to get to the bar. He was waylaid several times as friends stopped to greet him. Within a few minutes he returned with two frosty mugs of cold beer.

Bethany had barely had time to taste the brew when Joshua stood and offered her his hand. She didn't understand at first, then realized he was asking her to dance. The small dance floor was crowded when they moved to the edge of it. Joshua wrapped her in his arms, and they soon melted in with the others.

The minute Joshua had pulled her into his embrace, a wave of warmth had coursed through Bethany. She leaned her head back and looked up at him, realizing anew how much she loved this man.

He touched her cheek and his fingers felt like velvet against her cool skin. His lips were only a few inches away, and she longed with everything in her for him to kiss her again.

"Beth," he whispered urgently, "don't look at me like that."

Embarrassed, she lowered her gaze, all too aware of what he must be reading in her eyes.

"What the hell," he said, and moved ever so slightly to lift her chin and direct her mouth to his.

Bethany felt as if her bones were melting. She tasted the malt flavor of his beer as she opened her mouth to his. If his first kiss had been a sample, this second one was a feast. He slid his hands down her spine, molding her body intimately to his as he gave her a ruthless and plundering kiss. He moved his lips in eager exploration over hers until Bethany was convinced she would faint from the undiluted pleasure of it.

When he broke off the kiss, Bethany sagged against him, too weak to do anything but cling to the only solid thing in a world that was spinning out of control. She'd never wanted a man to make love to her more in her life. She shook with the urgent need that was building up inside her. Joshua nuzzled the side of her neck and then investigated the hollow of her throat with his tongue. She was gathered as close as humanly possible against him. When he kissed her again, his mouth was so hot it burned a trail all across her face.

"Let's get out of here," he whispered in a voice so thick and raspy she could hardly understand him.

She answered with a nod.

He kept her close to his side as he led them back to their table. They were about to leave when a tall dark man with a huge potbelly and a thick dark beard stopped him.

"You can't leave this place, Dizzy, without playing the blues."

"He's right, Dizzy," Bethany murmured, looking up at Joshua.

"Good to see you again, Fats." Joshua shook hands with the other man.

"You got your horn, brother?"

Joshua nodded reluctantly. "It's in the car."

"Get it."

Joshua looked almost apologetic as he led Bethany back to their table. "I'm sorry, sweetheart," he whispered.

She pressed her hands onto his shoulders and was so bold as to reach up and brush her lips across his. "I'm not. I want to hear you play."

The man Joshua had called Fats jumped onto the stage when Joshua reappeared. He carried his saxophone with him and Fats brought a bass trombone. The man who'd been playing the drums reappeared carrying a trumpet. The first couple of minutes were spent attaching reeds, checking valves and tooting a few notes. No one seemed to mind that the dancing had come to an abrupt halt. The room seemed to vibrate with a charged sense of anticipation.

Bethany sat back, watching Joshua and loving him more each minute. He stepped to the front of the stage and his gaze sought hers. The look he sent her way cut straight through her, and then he smiled and placed the instrument between his lips.

The blast of music split the air and was followed by shouts of encouragement from the audience. Soon the sounds of the other instruments joined Joshua: the piano, the trumpet, the trombone, each in turn.

Bethany couldn't have named the tune, didn't know that it had a title—the players weren't even following any sheet music. The sounds appeared improvisational as each player in his own time bent the notes his own way, twisting and turning, soaring and landing again. Bethany flew with them and she wasn't alone. Every patron in the club joined the flight, ascending with the music. The men played as if they were one, yet each separate. Bethany soaked in every note of Joshua's music, as if her heart had become a sponge meant only to take in this man and his love. She experienced the bright tension of the score as though each bar of music were meant for her and her alone. When they were finished, her eyes burned with unshed tears.

She remained in an almost dreamlike state when Joshua rejoined her. His face was close to hers and she could see the beads of perspiration that wetted his upper lip and brow. She raised her fingertip to his face, needing to touch him, needing to say what was inside her and unable to find the words to explain how his music had marked her soul.

Joshua gripped her hand with his own and kissed her fingertips.

"You like it?" he asked her, his gaze holding hers.

She nodded, and a tear escaped and ran down the side of her face. "Very much," she whispered.

"Bethany, listen." His hand continued to squeeze hers. "I'm going out of town next week."

She already knew about his trip to California.

"I haven't any right to ask this of you." He stopped and tangled his fingers in her hair. "I want you to come with me."

If he'd asked for her soul at that moment, she couldn't have refused him. "I'll come," she replied.

His eyes ate her up, seeming almost to ask her forgiveness. "Angie will be with me. She wants you to come and so do I."

Chapter Eight

When we're in California," Angie said thought-fully, sitting beside Bethany in the first-class section of the Boeing 737, "will you call me Millicent?"

"If you like."

The little girl nodded eagerly. "At least for the first day or two. I might want to change to Guinevere or Charmaine after that."

"I may slip up now and again," Bethany admitted, doing her utmost to remain serious. There were days she couldn't keep track of who *she* was, let alone a fun-loving ten-year-old.

"That's all right," Angie said, and went back to flipping through the pages of the flight magazine. She paused abruptly and looked back to Bethany. "Do you want me to call you Dominique? I could."

Bethany hesitated as if to give the child's offer serious consideration, then shook her head. "No thanks, sweetheart."

Joshua sat across the aisle from Angie and Bethany. His briefcase was open and he was busy reviewing some papers. His brow was creased in thick folds of concentration, his gaze intent. Bethany was convinced he'd long forgotten his daughter and his secretary, and her heart ached a little with the realization.

Inhaling a deep breath, Bethany pulled her eyes away from her employer and tried to involve herself in the plot of the murder mystery she was reading. It didn't work, although the author was one of her favorites. Instead, Sally's dire warning played back in her mind like a stubborn cassette tape that refused to shut off. It was happening again, her roommate had warned. Bethany was allowing Joshua to use her as a convenient babysitter. Bethany didn't want to believe that.

After Friday night, when Joshua had taken her to meet Cleo and she'd heard him play the saxophone at St. Peter's, Bethany had been convinced he felt something deep and meaningful for her. She wasn't so naive as to believe he loved her—that would have been too much to hope for so soon. But she couldn't deny Joshua had shared a deep personal part of himself with her and that went a long way toward making her forget she would be left solely in charge of Angie while Joshua tended to his business meetings.

"Daddy." Angie leaned across Bethany and called to her father. When he didn't immediately respond, his daughter took to waving her hand.

Joshua obviously didn't hear her or see her movements, or, if he did, he was too wrapped up in the report he was reading to break his concentration.

"What is it, Angie?" Bethany asked.

The ten-year-old leaned back in her seat. "How much longer? Will we be able to go to Disneyland today? I can hardly wait to see Mickey Mouse and Snow White."

Bethany checked her watch. "It'll be another couple of hours yet before we land."

"Oh." The small shoulders sagged with disappointment. "That long?"

"I'm afraid so."

"What about Disneyland?"

"There just won't be enough time after we leave the airport and check into the hotel."

"But Dad said we—"

"We'll see Mickey and Minnie first thing in the morning. I promise."

It looked for a moment as though Angie was going to argue with her, but the child apparently changed her mind and quietly settled back in her seat for a while. Then she squirmed once more.

"Is Dad going to be in meetings the whole time we're in California?"

Bethany nodded. She didn't like the idea of Joshua being constantly busy any better than Angie. When she'd originally made the arrangements for this trip, Joshua had requested that she schedule in a couple of days' free time so he could spend it with Angie, sightseeing. However, once Bethany had agreed to accompany him, the days he'd set aside to vacation had quickly filled up with appointments and business meetings. Now Joshua would be occupied the entire five days of their visit.

Their flight landed at LAX at five that evening, but by the time their luggage had been collected and the limousine had driven them into Anaheim, it was much later. Because of the time difference, Angie was overly tired, hungry and more than a little cranky.

Bethany hadn't fared much better during the long trip. Keeping Angie occupied had drained her completely. When Joshua had first asked her to accompany him, she'd been thrilled. Now she felt abused and sorely disappointed at the role she would be playing during the next few days. Her back was stiff, she was hungry, and she felt like Cinderella two nights after the ball, when her hair needed washing and there was a run in her panty hose.

Joshua had requested a suite for them close to the amusement park, where Bethany and Angie planned to spend a good deal of their stay. By the time they were settled in the hotel room, Angie was close to tears. Cranky because she was overly hungry, rummy because she was so tired and yet too excited to sleep.

It took Bethany the better part of an hour to convince the little girl to eat the hamburger Joshua ordered from room service. More time was spent persuading Angie that although it was still daylight, she really needed to rest. Angie was a little more cooperative once she took a bath. The ten-year-old climbed into bed with hardly a complaint and was asleep within five minutes.

Bethany felt as if she'd worked straight through a double shift when she joined Joshua in the suite's living room. She plopped herself down beside him on the davenport, slipped off her shoes and sagged against the back of the sofa, more exhausted than she could ever remember being in a long while.

Joshua set aside his papers and reached for her hand. His gaze revealed his appreciation. It was obvious from the moment Angie had started to whine in the airport when they'd landed that he wasn't going to be able to deal with his daughter patiently. He raised Bethany's hand to his mouth and brushed his lips over her knuckles. "I don't know what I'd do without you," he murmured.

A polite nod and a weak smile were all the response she could manage.

"I don't mean for you to work while we're here." He scooted closer to her and wrapped his arm around her, cupping her shoulder. "My intention had been to make this a vacation for you, as well ... I didn't realize Angie would be such a handful."

"She was just tired and cranky."

Joshua kissed the top of her head. "I know it was completely selfish of me to ask you to make this trip."

She didn't answer. Couldn't. Sally had been telling her what a fool she was from the minute Bethany had told her friend she would be traveling to California with Joshua and his daughter.

"The thought of spending five days without seeing you was more than I could bear."

Bethany so desperately wanted to believe him. She tucked her head under his chin and snuggled closer, almost too exhausted to appreciate the comfort his arms offered.

"I'm being unfair to you."

Bethany's eyes drifted shut when Joshua raised her chin and kissed her, his mouth brushing over hers in a swift sampling. She sighed and smiled contentedly. Tenderly Joshua smoothed wisps of hair away from her face and slowly glided his fingertips over her features.

"Such smooth skin," he whispered. "So warm and silky."

Bethany felt as if she'd gone ten rounds with Sugar Ray, but one kiss from Joshua wiped out everything but the cozy tranquil feeling of being held in his embrace. She slipped her left arm around his middle and tipped her head back, seeking more of his special brand of comforting.

When he didn't immediately kiss her again, Bethany's lashes fluttered open. What she saw in his eyes made her heart go still. Joshua was staring at her with such naked longing that she felt she would break out in a fever just looking at him. The words to tell him that she loved him burned on her lips, but she held them inside for fear of what voicing them would do to their relationship.

"Oh, Bethany, you are so beautiful." He whispered the words with such an intensity of emotion that she felt her heart melt like butter sitting too long in the hot sun. She wanted to tell him that it wasn't necessary for him to say those kind of things to her. He owned her heart, and had possessed it for three years.

His gaze held her a willing prisoner for what seemed like an eternity as he slowly slid his hand from the curve of her shoulder upward to her warm nape. He wove his fingers into her thick dark hair, and with his hand cupping the back of her head, he directed her mouth toward his. The kiss was full and lush. Rich. The man who was kissing her wasn't the arrogant man she worked with in the office. This was the same man who'd revealed a part of himself to her she was sure few others knew existed. The same man who had soared to unknown heights on the wings of a song he'd played just for her. The same man who gazed into her eyes and revealed such need, such longing that she would spend a lifetime remembering the pure desire she viewed there.

The shaking inside Bethany became so fierce that she raised her hand to grip Joshua's collar in a futile effort to maintain her equilibrium. Her flesh felt both hot and cold at the same time.

When he lifted his mouth from hers, Joshua drew in several ragged breaths. "Having you with me could end up being the biggest temptation of my life," he whispered in a raspy hoarse-sounding voice. He captured her hand and flattened her palm over his heart. "Feel what you do to me."

"I don't need to feel...I know, because you're doing the same thing to me."

"Bethany...listen, this isn't the right time for either of us and—"

She cut him off, not willing to listen to his arguments. All she longed to do was savor the sweet sensations he'd aroused in her with a single kiss. She slipped her hands around the thick cord of his neck and she offered him a slow seductive smile as she gently tugged at him and directed his mouth back to her own.

Joshua's eyes momentarily widened with surprise.

Bethany answered him with her own smile. Her lips parted, deepening the kiss. Joshua groaned and kissed her back as though he couldn't get enough of her. Bethany's breasts throbbed with the need for his touch, her nipples aching with anticipation. He didn't disappoint her and his hand lifted her sweater away from her abdomen. His fingers felt hot against her already flushed, heated skin. He sought her breast and when he found it, she sighed.

Joshua sighed, too. He circled her nipple lazily with his thumb until it grew so hard it ached almost painfully. She must have made some kind of sound, because Joshua reluctantly slid his mouth from hers.

Bethany protested with a soft moan, and when her lashes fluttered open she recognized his look of concern.

"Did I hurt you?"

"No." Embarrassed, she dropped her gaze. "It feels too good to have you touch me."

He closed his eyes like a man enduring the worst kind of torture. "Don't tell me that, Bethany."

"I can't help it."

He reached around and unclasped her bra. Bethany sank her teeth into her bottom lip as he lifted her sweater and pressed her back against the sofa. He kissed her once. Twice. Again. And while he kissed her, he worked magic with his hands on her breasts. Soon his mouth, moist and warm, replaced his fingers, and Bethany gasped as he closed his lips around her taut nipple, sucking and teasing. She arched her spine and felt herself slowly slipping beneath the waterline once more, willingly drowning in a deluge of naked desire.

The ringing sound didn't penetrate her conscience at first. But Joshua reacted almost immediately, jerking his head up and groaning aloud. A muffled curse followed.

"Yes?"

It wasn't until he spoke that Bethany realized Joshua had left her to answer the telephone. She blinked a couple of times, adjusting her eyes to the glaring light. Ill at ease, she sat upright, refastened her bra and pulled her sweater back into place.

"The flight was on time. Yes...yes, first thing in the morning. I'm looking forward to it. I've got those figures you asked to see. I think you'll be impressed with what's been happening the past couple of months. Yes, of course, eight. I'll be there."

Joshua spoke in crisp clear tones and no one would have guessed that only a few moments before he'd been making love to Bethany. The transformation from lover to businessman was as slick as ice on a country road.

It took Bethany several minutes to gather her composure enough to stand. Her knees felt shaky, and she was sure desire lingered in her expression. She brushed the hair out of her face and her hands trembled with the action. Joshua sat with his back to her, intent on his conversation. As far as he was concerned, Bethany could have been back in New Orleans. He had completely forgotten she existed.

She didn't wait until he was finished with his phone call. With her heart pounding like a battering ram against her rib cage, she walked across the floor, opened the door to the bedroom she would be sharing with Angie and slipped inside the darkened room. The

little girl was sound asleep, and Bethany didn't bother
to turn on any lights. She undressed silently, found her
way into the bathroom to brush her teeth and wash her
face. Then, she eagerly slipped between the clean
sheets. Within minutes Bethany felt herself sinking
into a black void of slumber, but not before she heard
Joshua's footsteps outside the bedroom door. He
paused, apparently thinking better of waking her, then
walked away.

Angie wore Mickey Mouse ears and carried a series
of colorful balloons, two huge stuffed animals and
other accumulated goodies the following afternoon
when Bethany opened the door to their hotel suite.

"Hi, Dad." Angie flopped down in a chair and let
out a giant whoosh of air. "Boy, am I tired."

Joshua grinned and sent a flashing query to Bethany. "How did you survive the day?"

"Great, I think. Only there isn't enough money in
the world to get me back on some of those rides."

"Bethany screamed all the way through the Magic
Mountain," Angie announced in a tattletale voice. "I
thought she had more guts than that."

"At least I didn't hide my eyes when I rode through
the Matterhorn."

"High places frighten me," Angie announced, accepting the ribbing good-naturedly.

Joshua leaned back in his chair and grinned at the
pair. "It looks to me like you've both had a grand
time."

"Did we ever. We saw Donald Duck and Goofy and
Snow White."

"Did you happen upon another Prince Charming?" Joshua asked. The gaze holding Bethany's was filled with curiosity.

"Unfortunately, no."

"A shame," he muttered, looking appropriately disappointed.

"The only white stallion I encountered was connected to an old-fashioned fire truck," she informed him, sharing his amusement. "I didn't have time to investigate further."

Joshua chuckled.

"How did your meeting go?" Bethany was all too aware that the future of Norris Pharmaceutical rested on the outcome of this business trip. She was worried for Joshua and prayed everything would go his way.

"The meeting went well." But he didn't elaborate.

"I'm starved."

Bethany nearly fell out of her chair at Angie's sudden announcement. "You just ate two hot dogs, cotton candy and a bag of peanuts."

"Can I help it?" the ten-year-old muttered. "I'm a growing child, at least that's what Mrs. Larson keeps telling me."

"And I'm one pooped adult." The thought of leaving the comfort of this hotel room on a food-seeking expedition so soon after arriving didn't exactly thrill Bethany.

"Is anybody interested in taking a swim?" Joshua asked, diverting his daughter's attention.

"Me." Instantly Angie was on her feet, eager to participate in anything that involved her father.

Bethany shook her head, too exhausted to move for the moment. "Maybe later—give me a few minutes to recuperate first." Her feet were swollen, although she'd worn a comfortable pair of old shoes. Her back ached and her head continued to spin from all the carnival rides Angie had insisted upon going on.

"I'm ready anytime you are, Dad," Angie cried out, and ran into the bedroom to change.

Joshua walked over to Bethany's side and bent down to lightly kiss her lips. "You look exhausted."

She smiled and nodded. "I'm too old to keep up with a ten-year-old."

"Go ahead and rest. I'll keep Angie occupied for the next hour or so."

"Bless you." Bethany wasn't teasing when she'd told Joshua how run-down she was. The energy level of one small girl was astonishing. They'd arrived at Disneyland when the amusement park opened first thing that morning and then had stayed for a full ten hours. On the monorail ride back to the hotel, Angie had casually announced that she intended to return to the park the following morning and then had wondered what there was to do that evening. All Bethany could think about was soaking in a hot tub and taking a long uninterrupted nap.

"We're off," Joshua said, coming out of his bedroom. He was wearing swimming trunks and had a thick white towel draped around his neck. He made such an attractive virile sight that Bethany nearly changed her mind about accompanying the pair.

"By, Bethany," Angie said, and waved, looking happy and excited. "Rest up, okay? Because there are a whole lot of things to do yet."

The opportunity for the little girl to spend time alone with her father was so rare. Bethany was pleased that Joshua was making the effort to fit Angie into his busy life.

The door closed and, with some effort, Bethany struggled to climb out of the chair. With her hand pressing against the small of her back, she made her way into the bedroom, deciding to forego a soak in the tub and, instead, rest her eyes a few minutes.

The next thing she knew an hour had slipped away, and she could hear whispered voices.

Angie stuck her head in the bedroom door and announced to her father, "Bethany's asleep."

Bethany's mouth formed a soft smile as she bunched up the feather pillow beneath her head and pulled the blanket more securely over her shoulders. She'd been having such a pleasant dream that she wanted to linger in the warm bed and relive a portion of it. In her mind, Joshua had been telling her how much he loved her. The scent of orange blossoms wafted through the air, and Bethany was convinced she could hear the faint strains of "The Wedding March."

"Dad," Bethany heard the ten-year-old whisper. "Have you ever thought about getting married again?"

Bethany's eyes popped open.

"No," Joshua muttered, and the tone of his voice told her that he found the subject matter distasteful.

"I've been thinking a lot about what it would be like to have a mother," Angie continued, apparently undaunted by the lack of enthusiasm in her father's voice.

Bethany lifted herself up on one elbow, wondering what she should do. If she were to make some kind of noise, then Angie and Joshua would know she was awake and end their talk. But it would be embarrassing to both Joshua and herself, and she wasn't eager to do that. However, if she sat and listened, she was going to regret it and feel guilty about listening in when their discussion clearly wasn't meant for her ears.

"Angie, listen to me—"

"You're supposed to call me Millicent," she interrupted, impatience ringing in her young voice.

"Millicent, Guinevere, whatever it is you want to be named this hour, I don't think my remarrying is a subject you and I should be discussing."

"Why not?"

Joshua apparently seemed to have some difficulty answering because silence filtered its way into the bedroom where Bethany lay listening. Muttering under her breath, she knew she should let them know she was awake. Obeying her conscience, she made a soft little noise that apparently went undetected.

"I've been thinking about what it would be like if you married Bethany," Angie continued. "I like her a whole bunch. She's such a lot of fun."

"Bethany's too young," Joshua answered shortly. "I'm nearly eleven years older than she is and—"

"Fiddlesticks," Angie cried. "I saw you kiss her once and you didn't seem to think she was too young for that!"

"When?" Joshua demanded, obviously disturbed by the information.

"A long time ago. I forget exactly when, but you did, and I saw you with my own two eyes."

Too young! Bethany mouthed the words in astonished disbelief. It was obvious Joshua was pulling excuses out of a hat in an effort to appease his daughter.

"You *did* kiss her, didn't you?"

"Yes," Joshua barked.

"And you liked it?"

"Angie." He paused, and Bethany could hear the sigh of frustration. "All right...Millicent, yes I *did* like it." The admission was ungracious, to say the least.

"Then I think you should marry Bethany."

"A whole lot more than liking the way someone kisses has to happen before a man considers marriage," Joshua explained with gruff impatience.

"It does?" Angie questioned. "Like what?"

"Things that a man doesn't discuss with his ten-year-old daughter."

"Oh," Angie muttered.

"Now for heaven's sake, don't say anything to Bethany about this or it'll make her uncomfortable." He paused, and from her position in the bedroom, Bethany could almost see Joshua pacing the floor. "You haven't talked to Bethany about this, have you?"

"No," Angie admitted eagerly. "I wanted to discuss it with you first. You told me I could talk to you about anything and I thought I should let you know that if you wanted to marry Bethany I'd like it real well. She'd make a great mother."

"Whatever you do, Angela, don't say anything to her!"

"I won't." Bethany heard Angie make a disparaging sound, but she wasn't sure what had prompted it. "Do you want any more children, Dad?"

"What?" The words seemed to explode from him.

"You know, another kid, like me?"

"I . . . I hadn't given it much thought. What makes you ask that?" It was clear from his tone of voice that Angie's questions were exasperating him.

"I don't know," Angie admitted, "except that if you and Bethany were to get married, then you'd probably have more children and I'd like that. I want a little sister and then a little brother."

"Did Bethany put you up to this?" Joshua's low voice was filled with suspicion.

Bethany was so outraged that she nearly flew out of bed to argue her own defense. How dare Joshua Norris think she would use his daughter to achieve her own ends. The very thought was despicable! If he believed for one second that she would resort to those kind of underhanded tactics, then he didn't know her at all, and that hurt more than anything else he'd said.

"Bethany doesn't know anything yet. I told you, I wanted to talk to you first."

"I see," Joshua muttered.

"You *will* think about marrying her, won't you, Dad?"

A year seemed to pass before Joshua answered. "Maybe."

Bethany's face was so hot she was sure she was running a high fever. Her heart constricted and she closed her eyes to the relentless pain that splashed over her.

After lingering in the bedroom another forty minutes, Bethany opened the door and stepped into the living area only to discover Angie and her father engrossed in a television movie.

"I didn't think you were ever going to wake up," Angie announced. "I'm starved, but Dad said we had to let you sleep."

"I'm sorry to keep you waiting," she said, having trouble keeping the hurt and resentment out of her voice. "You should have gone without me. I wouldn't have minded." The way she was feeling now, she didn't know that she could maintain her composure and not let Joshua know what she'd innocently overheard.

Angie didn't seem to notice a change in Bethany's attitude, but Joshua certainly did. He glanced her way and his gaze narrowed. "Are you feeling all right?"

"I'm fine," she lied.

"Good. I hope your healthy appetite is in place, because I've picked out an excellent Italian restaurant for dinner tonight."

"Hey, that sounds great," Angie said with a laugh, reaching out to claim Bethany's hand. "Come on, let's go, Dominique."

The remainder of their days ran together with all the different activities. Angie and Bethany visited Knott's Berry Farm, Universal Studios and several other tourist attractions. In the evenings, Joshua took charge of his daughter, finding ways of entertaining the preteen and relieving Bethany of the task. There were plenty of opportunities for Bethany to spend time alone with Joshua, but she avoided doing so as much as she could without being obvious about it.

The final night of their stay, Angie fell asleep in front of the television. Joshua carried the little girl into the bedroom and gently laid her on top of the mattress.

Bethany pulled the covers over the small shoulders and bent down to plant a swift kiss on the smooth brow. Joshua followed suit.

"I think I'll turn in myself," Bethany murmured, her gaze avoiding his.

Joshua arched his brows with surprise. "It's only a little after nine."

"It's . . . it's been a long day."

"Come on, I'll order us some wine. We have a lot to celebrate."

"Then the meetings went well for you?"

Joshua grinned and nodded.

Bethany was relieved for his sake. Now, perhaps, his life could return to normal, and her employer could go back to keeping regular hours instead of working day and night.

Joshua had a chilled bottle of Chablis sent to their room. The waiter opened it for them and poured.

"I have a one-glass limit," Bethany said, feeling awkward.

"You had more the other night, as I recall."

"Sure, but I'd just swan dived into Lake Pontchartrain, too, if you'll remember."

A smile broke out across his handsome features. "I'm not likely to forget."

They sat in the living room with the lights dimmed, looking out over the flickering lights of the city. Neither spoke for a long time.

"I want you to know how grateful I am that you accompanied me and Angie," Joshua started off by saying.

"The pleasure was all mine."

Joshua nodded.

"Since Angie's come to live with me, things have changed between us, haven't they?"

Bethany stared into her wine and nodded.

"I always thought of you as an efficient secretary, but bit by bit I've come to learn you're a warm, caring, nurturing woman."

"Thank you."

"I know you're attracted to me, Beth, and I haven't made any secret of the way I feel about you."

A droning sound seemed to attack her from all sides. He was going to ask her to marry him. She knew it as clearly as if he'd removed a diamond ring from inside his pocket and waved it under her nose. Angie had specifically requested her for a mother and Joshua was simply complying with the little girl's wishes.

She glanced up and tried to hold back the emotion that was clamoring for release.

Joshua's intense gaze held hers.

"I know this must be rather sudden, Beth, but I'd very much like you to consider marrying me. Will you?"

Chapter Nine

Bethany?"

With deliberately calculated movements, Bethany set aside her glass of Chablis. Her mind was spinning like a child's toy top, wobbling precariously now as the momentum was slowing. Her heart was shouting for her to accept Joshua's proposal, but her head knew it would be wrong.

"For a moment there, I actually thought I could do it," she whispered, feeling miserable and elated both at once.

Joshua regarded her soberly. "I don't understand."

She raised her hand to his face and lovingly pressed her palm against the side of his jaw. "I don't expect you to. I'm honored, Joshua, that you would ask me to be your wife, but the answer is no."

"No?" He looked positively stunned. "You didn't take time to think it over. You're turning me down? I thought . . . I'd hoped . . ."

Bethany hung her head. "I want so much more out of marriage than to be a replacement mother for a lonely little girl."

Joshua's brow folded into a deep dark frown. "What gives you the impression I'm asking you to be my wife because of Angie?"

"Joshua, please. . ."

"I want to know why," he demanded, his words as stiff and cold as frozen sheets.

If he was looking for an argument, Bethany wasn't going to provide one. She stood and offered him a sad but strong smile. "At least you didn't lie and tell me how much you love me. I've always admired that inherent streak of honesty in you. It's been ego shattering at times, but I've come to appreciate it." She swallowed at the painful lump that had formed in her throat. "Good night."

"Bethany." He ground out her name from between gritted teeth. "Sit down. It's obvious, if only to me, that we've got a good deal to discuss."

She shook her head. If they talked things over, she would be forced to tell him that she'd overheard his exchange with Angie, when his daughter had suggested Joshua marry her. To admit as much would be humiliating to them both.

"Good night, Joshua."

He clenched his jaw, and a muscle leaped at the side of his face. Bethany knew he was struggling to hold back his anger. Tears blurred her vision and she looked away, determined to leave the room with her pride, if nothing else, intact.

The return to New Orleans was as much of an ordeal for Bethany as the flight to California had been five days earlier. This time, however, Angie slept a good portion of the way. Joshua sat across the aisle from Bethany, and he might as well have been on a different airplane for all the attention he paid her. The silent treatment was exactly what Bethany had expected from him, but it still hurt. His protective shield was securely fastened in place, and with no apparent regret he'd shut her out of his heart and his life. Whatever possibility there had ever been for her to find happiness with Joshua Norris was now lost forever. He wouldn't ask her to marry him again and no doubt was sorry he'd done so the first time.

When they landed at Moisant International, Joshua saw to their luggage with barely more than clipped instructions to Bethany to wait with Angie for his return.

"Did you and my dad have a fight?" Angie asked, tucking her small hand in Bethany's and studying her carefully.

"Not an argument." Bethany knew it would be wrong to try to mislead Joshua's daughter into believing everything was as it had been earlier in the week.

"How come ever since we left California, you look like you want to cry?"

The best answer Bethany could come up with was a delicate shrug, which she knew wasn't going to appease a curious ten-year-old.

"Dad's been acting weird, too," Angie murmured thoughtfully, glancing toward her father, who was waiting for their suitcases to circle the carousel. "He hardly talks to you anymore." She paused, as though waiting for Bethany to respond, and when she didn't, Angie added, "Dad and I had a long talk, and we decided that it would be a good idea if you two got married." She slapped her hand over her mouth. "I wasn't supposed to tell you that."

"I already know," Bethany said, feeling more miserable by the minute.

"You're going to marry Dad, aren't you?" Eyes as round as grapefruit studied her, waiting for her response.

"No." The lone word wavered and cracked on its way out of Bethany's throat. She loved Angie almost as much as she did Joshua, but she couldn't marry him to satisfy his little girl.

"You *aren't* going to marry my dad?" If Joshua had looked stunned when she'd refused his proposal, it was a minor reaction compared to the look of disbelief Angie gave her. "You really aren't?"

"No, sweetheart, I'm not."

"Why not?"

Bethany brushed the soft curls away from the distraught young face and squatted down to wrap her arms around Angie, who wanted to be called Millicent. "I love you both so much," she whispered brokenly.

"I know that." Ready tears welled in Angie's eyes. "Don't you want to be my new mom?"

"More than anything in the world."

"I don't understand..."

Bethany didn't know any way to explain it. "Your father will find someone else, and . . ."

"I don't want anyone else to be my mother. I only want you."

Fiercely Bethany hugged the little girl close and Angie's tears soaked through her silk blouse. "I . . . have to go now," Bethany whispered unevenly, watching Joshua make his way toward them, carrying their suitcases. "Goodbye, Millicent."

"But, Bethany, what about . . ."

Remaining there and listening to Angie's pleas was more than Bethany could bear. She lifted the suitcase out of Joshua's hand without looking at him and hurriedly walked away.

"Bethany, don't go," the little girl cried. "Don't go . . . please, don't go."

The words ripped through Bethany's heart, but she didn't turn around. Couldn't. Tears streaked her face as she rushed outside the terminal and miraculously flagged down a taxi.

"You honestly refused Joshua's proposal," Sally demanded, pacing in front of Bethany like an angry drill sergeant. "You were delirious with fever at the time and didn't know what you were saying. Right?"

"No, I knew full well what turning him down would mean."

"Are you nuts, girl?" Sally asked, slapping her hands against the side of her legs and stalking the area like a caged panther. "You've been in love with J. D. Norris for years."

"I know."

"How can you be so calm about this?" Her hands made a hitting noise against her thighs a second time.

Bethany shrugged, not exactly sure herself. "I wouldn't even mention it except I'm going to be looking for another job right away. As soon as you realized what I was doing, you'd hound me with questions until I ended up confessing everything anyway."

"He fired you!"

"No," Bethany whispered. But she couldn't continue to work with Joshua. Not now. It would be impossible for them both.

"I thought you were crazy about this guy."

"I am." Crazy enough to want the best for him. Crazy enough to want him to find his own happiness. Crazy enough to love him in spite of everything. For Joshua to marry her to provide a mother for his little girl wouldn't be right. "When he first asked me, I honestly thought I could do it. The words to tell him how much I wanted to share his life were right there on the tip of my tongue, but I had to force myself to swallow them." It had been the most difficult task of Bethany's life, but she didn't feel noble. Her emotions ran toward sad and miserable. Perhaps someday she would be able to look back and applaud her gallantry. But not now, and probably not for a long time.

"But why would you refuse him?" Sally was looking at her as though it would be a good idea to call in a psychiatrist.

"He doesn't love me."

"Are you so sure of that?" Her roommate eyed her carefully, clearly unconvinced.

"I'm positive."

"Well, big deal! He'd learn to in a year or so. Some of the greatest marriages of all time were based on something far less than true love."

"I know that, but the risk is too high. Joshua might come to love me later, but what if he doesn't? What if he woke up a year from now and realized he deeply loved another woman? I know Joshua. I know that he'd calmly accept his sorry fate and let the one he really loved walk out of his life."

"What about *your* life?"

Bethany ran her hand down her skirt, smoothing away an imaginary wrinkle. The deliberate movement gave her time to examine her thoughts. "I'm not being completely unselfish in all this. Yes, I love him, and yes, I love Angie, but I have a few expectations when it comes to marriage, too. When and if I ever marry, I want my husband to be as crazy in love with me as I am with him. When he looks at me, I want him to feel that his life would be incomplete without me there to share it with him."

"So you've decided to give J.D. your two week-notice first thing Monday morning?"

Bethany nodded. "You should be glad, Sal. You've been after me to do it for months."

"I don't feel good about this," Sally muttered, folding her arms over her chest, her brow furrowed with a frown. "Not in the least bit."

Monday morning, Bethany had her letter of resignation typed before Joshua arrived at the office. The paper was on his desk waiting for him.

She gave him a minute to find it before entering the executive suite. Joshua was sitting at his desk reading it when she delivered his coffee to him and handed him the morning mail.

"I hope two weeks is sufficient notice?" she asked politely, doing her utmost to remain outwardly calm and composed.

"It's plenty of time," he said without looking in her direction. "I'd like you to review the applications yourself, decide upon two or three and I'll interview the ones you feel are best qualified."

"I'll contact personnel right away."

"Good."

She turned to leave, following his instructions regarding the mail, but Joshua stopped her. "Miss Stone."

"Yes?"

His gaze held hers for an agonizingly long moment. "You've been an excellent secretary... I'm sorry to lose you."

"Thank you, Mr. Norris." She hesitated before turning and walking out of his office. She longed to ask him about Angie but knew it would be impossible. She hadn't contacted the little girl, believing a clean break would be easier for them both. But Bethany hadn't counted on it being this difficult, or how much she would miss the little ray of sunshine who was Joshua's daughter.

A week passed, and Bethany was astonished that she and Joshua could continue to work together so well. They rarely spoke to each other, except for a few brief sentences that were required to accomplish the everyday business of running the office. Bethany was miserable, but she knew she was right, and however painful it was for now, the hurt would eventually go away.

At Joshua's instructions, she reviewed several applications personnel sent up. She sorted out three who she felt would nicely fill her role with Norris Pharmaceutical. Joshua interviewed all three and chose a matronly woman in her early fifties as her replacement. For the next week, Bethany worked closely with the woman so the transition would be as smooth as possible.

On her last day, Joshua called her into his office, thanked her for three years of loyal service and handed her a bonus check. Bethany gasped when she saw the amount, pressed her lips together and calmly said, "This is too much."

"You earned it, Miss Stone."

"But..."

"For once, Miss Stone, kindly accept something without arguing with me."

It would do little good anyway, so she nodded and whispered brokenly, "Thank you, Mr. Norris."

"Have you found other employment?" he asked her unexpectedly, delaying her departure.

She shook her head. She hadn't taken the time to look. With everything else going on in her life, another job didn't seem all that important.

"I wish you the very best, Miss Stone."

"You too, Mr. Norris." She couldn't say anything more, fearing her voice would crack. As it was, tears hovered just below the surface. "Thank you, again."

"Goodbye, Bethany."

She lowered her gaze and worried the corner of her lower lip. "Goodbye, Joshua."

With that, she turned and walked out of his life.

"Well, did you get the job?" Sally asked her one afternoon when she arrived home from work.

The whole day had been gorgeous and sunny and Bethany knew she should be like everyone else in the city and want to enjoy this unusual display of summerlike weather. Instead she was inside, reading a book.

"The position was offered to someone else." For emphasis, Bethany shook her head. She'd gone in for an interview and was pleased for the woman who got the job since she so obviously wanted it. Bethany couldn't have cared less.

"You don't look all that disappointed."

"Sally, I don't know what's wrong with me," she said on the tail end of a drawn-out sigh. "I don't care if I ever find another job. All that interests me is sleeping, and if I'm not doing that, I'm reading. I've read more books in the past month than I did all the year before."

"You're escaping."

"I know that." Bethany didn't need her friend to tell her the obvious. It didn't hurt as much when her face was buried in a good book—as long as it wasn't a romance—reading about true love wasn't exactly her favorite topic at the present time. Murder mysteries appealed to her far more. Bloody battered bodies— that sort of thing.

Sally looked at her watch and gasped. "I've got to change and get ready," she said, and hurried toward her bedroom.

"For what?" Bethany asked, following her friend.

Sally blushed. "Jerry and I are going on a picnic."

"You've been out with him every night for the past week."

"I know," Sally admitted, and sighed sheepishly. "I'm in love, and I'll tell you right now—if Jerry Johnson proposed to me, I'd accept."

Bethany faked a pain-filled cry at the low unexpected blow and turned away. "May your first son grow up to style women's hair."

Sally chuckled, tossed her shirt on her unmade bed and reached for her jeans. "You'll be all right, won't you?"

"I'll be fine. I stopped off at the library on my way back to the apartment. I've got enough reading material to last most people a lifetime. But at the rate I've been going I'll be done with this stuff in a week." Her small attempt at humor fell decidedly flat.

Being the true friend, Sally rolled her eyes toward the ceiling and mumbled something under her breath about misguided love and Bethany not knowing what was good for her.

The apartment felt empty with Sally gone. Bethany figured she might as well get used to it. The way her roommate's romance was progressing, Sally could well end up marrying the young attorney before the end of the summer.

About seven, the doorbell rang. Bethany climbed off the sofa to answer it, unsure who it could be.

"Joshua?" She pulled open the door and nearly sagged against it. Bethany was never more shocked to see anyone in her life.

"Is this a bad time? I know I should have phoned, but I was detained and..." He let the rest of what he was saying dwindle off.

"No, I'm not doing anything important. Please come in." She stepped aside in order for him to enter the apartment.

Bethany hurried ahead of him and picked up an empty soda can and a banana peel, feeling embarrassed and foolish. "Sit down." She gestured toward the davenport. "Can I get you something to drink?"

"No, thank you."

She deposited the garbage in the kitchen and rushed back into the living room, holding her hands behind her back in nervous agitation. "Is something wrong at the office? I mean... I'd be happy to help in any way I could."

"Everything's fine."

Alarm filled Bethany when she realized there would only be one reason Joshua would come to her. "It's Angie, isn't it? She's had an accident—"

"No. Angie's doing very well. She misses you, but that's to be expected."

Relief flooded through her and she sagged into the chair across from Joshua.

He sat uncomfortably close to the end of the cushion on the sofa. "The purpose of my visit is to see if you'd found another job."

"Not yet...." She couldn't very well announce that she'd taken to job hunting the way a cat does to water. If she spent the rest of her life reading and eating bananas, she would be content.

"I see." He braced his elbows against his knees and laced his fingers together. "I thought I might be able to help."

"Help?" It came to her then. The purpose behind his visit should have been as clear as Texas creek water. Anyone but a blind fool would have figured out that Joshua wanted to hire her as a baby-sitter for Angie. If he couldn't convince her to marry him then he would no doubt be willing to pay her top dollar for her child-rearing services.

"Yes, help," Joshua said, ignoring her look of outrage. "I have certain connections and I may be able to pull a few strings for you, if you'd like."

"Strings?" Bethany repeated. So he hadn't come because of Angie. She narrowed her gaze suspiciously, not knowing what to believe.

"Is something wrong?"

"No," she returned quickly.

"I understand Hal Lawrence of Holland Mills is looking for an executive secretary, and I'd be happy to put in a good word for you."

"That would be thoughtful."

"I'll call him first thing in the morning then."

"Thank you." Bethany continued to watch him closely, unsure what to make of his offer.

Joshua stood and the action was reluctant. "I was wondering..." he said after an awkward moment.

"Yes?" she prompted, tilting her head back so far she nearly toppled in her effort to look up at him.

Joshua jammed his hands inside his pant pockets, then jerked them out again. "What makes you so certain I don't love you?"

Briefly Bethany toyed with the idea of asking him outright what he *did* feel for her but was hesitant to do so.

"Bethany," he said softly, "I asked you a question."

"I wasn't asleep," she answered weakly, her voice trapped and unstable.

"Asleep?" he demanded. "What in the hell are you talking about?"

"The first day in California," she continued, refusing to meet his impatient gaze. "I overheard Angie ask you if you'd ever thought of remarrying."

"Ah," Joshua whispered, sounding almost relieved.

Bethany didn't like his attitude. "Perhaps more important, Joshua Norris, I heard your answer."

"You're basing everything on that?"

"As I recall, Joshua, you seemed to think I'd put her up to the questioning. That was the worst of it . . . that you'd assume I would use Angie that way."

"I knew you wouldn't do that—you must have misunderstood me."

"Perhaps." She was willing to concede that much. "Even if I hadn't heard you talking to Angie . . . that night you ordered the wine . . ."

"Yes?" He was clearly growing impatient with her, shifting his weight from one foot to the other.

"You didn't tell me how you felt then, either. I may have been too willing to jump to conclusions, but it seems to me that if you honestly love me then that would've been the time to tell me as much."

"Did it ever occur to you that a man wouldn't ask a woman to marry him without feeling something for her?"

"Oh, I'm sure you do...did," she corrected stiffly. "I haven't worked with you all these years without knowing how you operate. Unfortunately, I want more."

Joshua paced back and forth a couple of times before sitting back down again. He leaned forward, braced his elbows on his knees and exhaled sharply.

"The word *love* frightens me," he said after a moment, his gaze leveled on the worn carpeting. "I loved Angie's mother, but it wasn't enough. Within a year after we were married, Camille was discontented. I thought a baby would keep her occupied, but she didn't want children. I should have listened to her, should have realized then that nothing I would ever do would be enough. But I was young and stupid and I loved her too much. Angie was unplanned and Camille had a terrible pregnancy. When she was about five months along, she moved to New York to be with her family. Camille never cared for Angie, had never wanted to be a mother. Whatever instincts women are supposed to have with a baby were missing with her. Her mother was the one who took care of Angie from the very first.

"Camille insisted she needed a vacation to recover after Angie's birth and stayed with her parents while I took what time I could to fly between the two cities.

"Angie was only a few months old when Camille asked for the divorce. She was in love with another man." He paused and wiped a hand over his face, as if the action would clean the slate of that miserable portion of his life. "Apparently Camille had been involved with him for months after she moved to New York—even before Angie was born."

The pain in his eyes was almost more than Bethany could stand. She stood, walked over to the sofa and sat beside him. Joshua clasped her hand in his.

"She died in a freak skiing accident a few months later."

"Oh, Joshua, I'm so sorry." She closed her eyes and pressed her forehead against his upper arm.

"Why?" he asked, almost brutally.

"Because . . . because she broke your heart."

"Yes, she did," he admitted reluctantly. "I'd assumed I was immune to love until Angie came to live with me. I felt safe from emotional attachments."

A tear rolled down the side of Bethany's pale face. If Joshua was hoping to convince her he loved her, he'd failed by dragging his daughter into the conversation. Everything he was saying now only went toward proving her point.

Joshua paused and gently wiped the moisture from her cheek. He gripped her shoulders then, turned her in his arms and firmly planted his mouth over hers. His kiss was unlike any they'd shared in the past. His mouth moved urgently in a ruthless plundering as if to punish her for the misery she'd caused them both. He slid his hands from her shoulders to her back, crushing her breasts into his warm sturdy chest. This was a trial by fire, and Bethany felt herself lose control, surrendering all she had, all she would ever be to Joshua. Like a hothouse flower peeling open its petals, Bethany blossomed under Joshua's expert lovemaking.

When he'd finished, Bethany's body was aflame and trembling. He straightened and sucked in deep gulps of air. His gaze was narrowed and clouded.

"Honest to God, Bethany, if this isn't love, I don't know what is."

With that, he stood and walked out.

Bethany was too weak to do anything more than lift her hand to stop him. Her voice refused to go higher than a weak whisper when she called out to him.

The front door slammed, and Bethany sat there for a full minute, too bemused to do anything except breathe. Gradually the beginnings of a smile came. A shaky kind of hopeful happiness took control. Joshua had never been a man to express his emotions freely. Maybe, just maybe, she'd misjudged him. He'd swallowed his considerable pride and come to her, and although he hadn't admitted that he loved her, he'd come close. In thinking about their conversation, Bethany realized she hadn't given him the opportunity to tell her how he felt.

An hour later the phone rang. Bethany reached for it and was pleasantly surprised to hear Joshua answer her greeting.

"Oh, Joshua, I'm so pleased you called. I've been thinking ever since you left and—"

"Bethany, have you heard from Angie?"

"No," she admitted, a little hurt by the cutting edge of his voice.

"You're sure she hasn't called you?"

"Joshua, of course I'm sure." The implication that she would lie to him was strong and she didn't like it in the least.

"Joshua, what's going on?"

A long moment passed before he spoke. "Angie's missing. Mrs. Larson saw her after school, but she hasn't been seen by anyone since."

The memory of the little girl telling her how much she enjoyed swimming and how she wished her father would go with her more often rang in Bethany's mind like a funeral gong.

"Joshua," she whispered through her panic. The day was gorgeous. Sally and Jerry were on a picnic. "Could Angie have gone to the lake?"

Chapter Ten

Bethany didn't bother to ring the doorbell to Joshua's Lake Pontchartrain home. She barreled through the front door, breathless and so frightened she could barely think clearly. Her mind continued to echo Angie's words about wanting to swim alone in the lake like ricocheting bullets, and the fear Bethany experienced with each beat of her heart was debilitating.

"Joshua," she cried, stepping into the living room.

He walked out of his den, and his eyes carried a look of agony of the damned. "She hasn't been seen or heard from since right after school...there's no evidence she went down to the lake. At least none that Mrs. Larson or I could find...."

Tears blurred Bethany's vision as she rushed across the room and into Joshua's arms. She wasn't sure what had driven her there—whether it was to lend comfort or receive it, she didn't know. Perhaps both.

His chest felt warm and solid as she pressed her face into it and breathed in deeply in an effort to regain her equilibrium.

Joshua held on to her desperately, burying his face in the gentle slope of her throat, drinking in her strength, her courage, her love.

The thought passed though Bethany's mind with laser swiftness that this was perhaps the first time Joshua had ever truly needed her.

"I think she may have run away," he confessed in a voice that rocked with emotion. "She told me once that she'd thought about it. There's no other plausible explanation."

"But why?"

Joshua dropped his arms and momentarily closed his eyes. "I'm rotten father material. From the first, I've done everything wrong. I love Angie, but I'm just not a good parent. God knows I've—"

"Joshua, no!" Bethany reached for his hand, holding it between both of her own and pressing it to her cheek. "That's not true. You've been wonderful, and if you've made mistakes, that's understandable...really. No parent is perf—" Bethany stopped speaking abruptly, cutting off the last word. Her eyes grew round as the horror of her actions struck her between the solar plexus...the consequences of refusing Joshua's proposal. "It's me, isn't it? Angie's... been upset because I haven't talked to her since...the California trip. She assumed I turned you down because of her, and, Joshua...oh, Joshua, that just isn't so." She took a step away from him and folded her hands over her middle as the reality burned through her like hot oil. "That's...that's why you came to see me today, isn't it? You were worried then that something like this would happen, and you thought..." Everything was so amazingly clear now.

"No," Joshua said gruffly, regretfully. "I'm not going to lie. Angie and I *did* discuss the matter before I proposed, but she accepted your decision..." He paused and looked away, his face tight and proud. "In fact, she took it better than I did." He turned away and raked his hand impatiently through his hair. "Telling you this no doubt confirms the worst."

"Confirms the worst," she repeated. "I don't understand."

"You chose to believe I asked you to be my wife because I was looking for a mother for Angie."

Bethany couldn't help thinking exactly that. But it wouldn't have mattered if Joshua truly loved her. She looked at him, her soul in her eyes. "That's true, isn't it, about wanting me to be a mother to Angie?"

His shoulders sagged a little, and a sad smile bounced against the edges of his mouth but didn't catch. "I can't say the way Angie loves you didn't weigh into my decision, and I suppose that condemns me all the more. But my daughter loves Mrs. Larson, too, and the thought of marrying her never once entered my mind."

Bethany's heart began to do a slow drumroll.

"I know you probably don't believe this, but I *do* love you, Bethany. I have for weeks."

His words had the most curious effect upon her. She stared at him, her blue eyes as wide as the Mississippi River. She was too stunned to react for a wild second, then she calmly, casually burst into tears.

It was clear from the way Joshua jerked forward and then quickly retreated that he didn't know what to do.

"Then why didn't you once so much as hint at the way you felt?" she wailed.

"I did," he countered. "Every way I knew how."

"But..."

"You weren't exactly a boiling pot of information yourself," he told her.

"You knew how I felt." If everyone at Norris Pharmaceutical right down to the newest member of the typing pool realized she loved Joshua Norris, it was unlikely that he'd failed to notice.

"Yes," he admitted reluctantly. "I realized it the evening we bumped into each other at Charley's... the night Angie arrived."

That soon. Bethany gulped at the information. Her thoughts were interrupted when a glimpse of color flashed in her peripheral vision. She turned abruptly to see the tail of a flowered summer shirt disappear into Joshua's sloop. Angie.

"Joshua..." She folded her fingers around his forearm and pointed toward his sailboat moored at the end of the long dock at the edge of the lake. "I just saw Angie."

"What?" He was instantly alert. "Where?"

"She's hiding in the sailboat."

"What the bloody hell! Why?"

"I...don't know."

"Well, I intend to find out. Right now." He jerked open the French patio door hard enough to pull it off its hinges.

"Joshua..." Bethany ran after him. "Calm down."

"I will once she's been properly disciplined." Bethany was forced to run to keep up with his lengthy strides.

He marched onto the dock like an avenging warlord. "Angela Catherine," he shouted, and the sound of his anger was furious.

The top of a small brown head appeared, followed slowly by a round pair of dark eyes.

"Angie! How could you have worried us this way?" Bethany cried, and covered her mouth with her hand, both relieved and upset.

"Hi, Dad." Hesitantly Angie stood and lifted her hand to greet him. "Hi, Bethany."

"Come out of that boat this minute, young lady," Joshua demanded.

"Okay." As though she'd recently returned from a world tour, Angie retrieved a pillowcase stuffed full of her clothes and tossed that to her father. She handed Bethany a week's supply of snack foods jammed to the top in another. Joshua's daughter made a show of climbing over the side of the sailboat and onto the dock.

Bethany had to give the kid credit for sheer courage.

"I suppose I'm going to get the spanking of my life," she said, calmly accepting her punishment. "I don't mind, really." She squared her shoulders and offered her father a brave smile.

"Go to your room and wait for me there," Joshua ordered.

"Okay." The ten-year-old glanced from her father to Bethany and back again. "Can I ask Bethany something first?"

Joshua expelled his breath in a burst of impatience and nodded.

"Are you going to marry my Dad and me?"

"Angela Catherine, go to your room." Joshua pointed in the direction of the house. "Now!"

The young head dropped. "All right."

The two adults followed Angie through the patio doors. Bethany deposited the pillowcase full of food onto the living room carpet and rubbed her palms back and forth as she gathered her thoughts.

"I was right," Joshua said, looking pale and greatly troubled. "Angie had decided to run away."

"I don't think she was planning to go far."

Joshua sat on the edge of the sofa and dragged his hands over his face. "But why?" He tossed the question to Bethany and seemed to expect an answer.

"I . . . I don't know."

"Angie and I have been closer than ever the past few weeks," Joshua admitted, and every feature of his handsome face revealed his bewilderment. "I can hardly believe she would do this."

Not able to understand it herself, Bethany sat beside Joshua, her legs weak with relief that they'd found the little girl.

"I'm not cut out for this parenting business. I've done everything wrong from the minute that child was born," Joshua muttered, his discouragement palpable.

"I sincerely hope you don't mean that," Bethany whispered, and rested her head against the outside curve of his shoulder.

He turned to her then, his gaze narrow and curious.

"I'd like us to have a family someday," she whispered, gladly answering the question in his eyes.

"You would?" His voice was taut, strangled and nothing like normal.

"Yes," she answered with a short nod. "Two, I think. Three, if you want."

"Bethany, oh dear Lord." His eyes went dark, the pupils dilating as he continued to stare at her with his mouth gaping open. "You mean it, don't you?"

"Of course I mean it! I love you so much."

His eyes dropped closed, as though he had paused to savor each syllable of each word. "Then you *do* plan to marry me?"

"I'd prefer to before the children are born," she answered with a soft teasing smile.

Joshua pulled her into his arms and kissed her then with a hungry desperation, rubbing his mouth back and forth over hers, sampling her lips as a man would enjoy an expensive rare delicacy.

Bethany wound her arms around his neck and leaned into him, offering him everything. He broke off the kiss, but his lips continued a series of soft nibbles down the side of her face.

"That night at Charley's," he whispered.

"Yes..."

"Having you come up to me at the bar, your eyes so full of concern, your love so open...it shook me to the core. I'd worked with you all that time, and I'd never seen you as anything more than an excellent secretary."

"I know," she said with a tinge of remembered frustration. Bethany ran her fingers through his hair and down the side of his face to his neck, reveling in the freedom to touch him. "I was ready to give you my notice then. I thought my love for you was completely useless."

"I think I realized that, too...and for a time I thought it would be for the best if you *did* find other employment. Then you were gone that one day and the office seemed so empty and dark without you. I realized that if you left, nothing would ever be the same in my life again, and I couldn't let you go."

"Oh, Joshua."

"My reasoning wasn't so selfless," he admitted. "I didn't intend to fall in love with you...that took me by surprise. The day you fell in the lake, I knew it was useless to pretend anymore. Oh my beautiful, adorable Bethany, what a pitiful sight you made that afternoon, with water dripping at your feet."

She groaned at the memory.

"But you held your head high and walked out of that water as though drenching yourself in it had been your intention all along. I stood on the shore and knew right then and there it wasn't going to do the least bit of good to fight you any longer. I was going to love you all the days of my life."

"The prince..." She lifted her face to watch him, needing to know if the man who'd swept her into his arms at the Mardi Gras parade had been Joshua.

"Yes?"

"It was you, wasn't it?"

He looked sheepish and a little embarrassed when he nodded. "I can't believe I did anything so crazy... it's not like me, but I wanted to kiss you again, needed to because I didn't know if I'd ever get the chance with what was happening with the—"

"But why?" she interrupted.

He took her hand and lifted it to his mouth. "You were aware of only a fraction of what was going on with the company at the time. I nearly lost it, Bethany, nearly lost everything. I was in the middle of the biggest financial struggle of my life. The timing for falling in love couldn't have been worse."

"Telling me you loved me would have gone a long way, Joshua Norris."

He grinned. "Now perhaps... but not last month. Everything I had in the world was on the line. I had to deal with the financial hassles before I could pursue our relationship."

"I could have helped." She wasn't sure how, but surely there would have been some way.

"You couldn't—there wasn't anything you could have done. I knew if I lost Norris Pharmaceutical, I'd be losing you, too."

"How can you say that? I would never have left you...."

"I know." He bunched her face between his hands and kissed her again. "I died a thousand deaths when I heard Sally arrange that date for you."

"She... she was convinced you were using me."

Joshua leaned his forehead against hers. "As a baby-sitter? There wasn't a single moment I needed you to watch Angie—they were all excuses, each instance, to have you close, to spend time with you. I thanked God for the excuse. I was so afraid I was going to lose you to someone else while I was forced to deal with the second takeover bid. I invented reasons to keep you close."

"But in California, when Angie suggested you marry me, you didn't sound pleased with the prospect."

"I wish to God you'd been asleep that day," he admitted with a frown. "Everything was still up in the air—I'd only met one day with Hillard and his group. I loved you then, Bethany, but a man can't come to a woman without something to offer her."

"But you seemed to think I'd put Angie up to that conversation."

He grinned. "If I *did* suggest that, then it was with a prayer and a smile because I wanted you so much, and I was hoping you wanted me, too. I could hardly stand the wait myself. The day the negotiations were finalized, I asked you to marry me. Delaying it even a minute longer was intolerable."

"But you didn't tell me you loved me that night and..."

"Good Lord, Bethany, I was a nervous wreck. Surely you noticed? I'd been as jumpy as a toad all evening, waiting to get you alone and then, when I finally managed, you didn't seem the least bit inclined to want my company. All day I'd been rehearsing what I wanted to say and instead I blurted out the question like a college freshman. You could have bowled me over with a Ping-Pong ball when you refused."

"I thought..."

He interrupted by sliding his mouth over hers. "I know exactly what twisted thoughts you'd been harboring...and I'll admit my pride took a beating that night and all the nights that followed. It wasn't easy to come to you this afternoon, but I've realized my life isn't going to be worth a damn without you."

"Oh, Joshua." Tears of tenderness filled her eyes and a precious kind of sweetness pierced her heart. She found his mouth with hers and kissed him with all the bursting aching love stored so restlessly there.

"And then I blew everything a second time and came home to discover Angie was missing."

At the mention of his daughter, Bethany straightened. "I think we should talk to her. Together."

"All right," he agreed, standing. His hand was linked with hers as he led her down the hallway to the downstairs bedrooms.

Joshua rapped at Angie's bedroom door and then let himself inside. Angie sat on the edge of the mattress, her head bowed and her hands clasped in her lap.

"All right, young lady, what do you have to say for yourself?"

"Nothing."

The word was so low Bethany had to strain to hear it.

"Surely you realized how worried Bethany and I would be?"

Angie nodded several times, still not looking at them.

"If you knew that, then what possible reason could you have for doing something like this?"

Two small shoulders jerked up, then sagged.

"Are you unhappy, sweetheart?" Bethany asked.

The little girl shook her head. "I like living here better than anyplace in the world."

"Then why would you want to run away?" Joshua demanded.

A short pulsating silence followed.

"So Bethany would come."

"I beg your pardon?" Joshua advanced a step toward his daughter.

"So Bethany would come," Angie repeated a little louder.

"I heard you the first time, but I don't understand your reasoning . . . not in the least."

"When you talked to me last week, you said we might have been hoping for too much with Bethany, because she didn't want to marry you, and I knew that was wrong. I knew she loved you and I know she loves me, so I figured if something bad happened, then she'd come and you two would talk and then maybe she'd want to marry us."

Bethany gasped at the logic, because essentially that was what had happened.

"Your intentions may have been good, but what you did was very wrong."

"I know." For the first time Angie raised her eyes to meet her father's. "Can you let me know how many swats I'm going to get? If you tell me that, I can hold back and not cry."

Joshua seemed to be contemplating that when Angie interrupted him.

"I saw Bethany from the sailboat and she looked real worried, and then I saw you talking and I couldn't hardly wait to hear what you said, so I snuck out of the boat and came to the patio to listen." A smile as wide as the Grand Canyon broke out across the little girl's face. "I wasn't sure, but it sounded like Bethany wants us."

"Oh, sweetheart, I've always wanted you." Bethany wasn't sure if Joshua would approve of her comforting Angie, but she wrapped her arms around the little girl and hugged her close.

"You're going to marry us?"

Bethany nodded eagerly.

"Oh, good!" She beamed a smile at her father and added, "You can give me as many swats as you want, and I bet I won't even feel them."

Bethany was just preparing to move into the role of stepmother, and she didn't want to cross Joshua, but she couldn't bear the thought of Angie being spanked. She tried to tell him as much with her eyes.

He answered her with a look of his own, cleared his throat and announced, "Seeing that everything's worked out for the best, I believe we can forego the spanking."

"We can?" Angie all but flew off the bed. Her arms groped for Joshua's waist, and she hugged him with all her might.

"However, you caused Bethany, Mrs. Larson and several others a good deal of concern. You're restricted for the next two weeks, young lady."

Some of the delight drained out of Angie's eyes. She sank her teeth into her lower lip and nodded. "I won't ever do it again, I promise. I . . . I thought it would be fun, but it wasn't. I was bored to tears."

"Good. I sincerely hope you've learned your lesson."

"Oh, I did." She slipped one arm around Bethany's waist, and the other around her father, and stood between the two adults. "We're going to have such a good life together."

"I think so, too," Bethany agreed.

"Especially after the other kids arrive," Angie said, looking vastly pleased with herself. "I want a sister first, okay? And then a brother."

Joshua's gaze reached out to Bethany and wrapped her in an abundance of warmth. "I'm more than willing to do my part to complete the picture."

Bethany couldn't have looked away to save the world from annihilation. Tears of joy welled up in her eyes, and she nodded. "Me, too."

Angie released a long slow sigh. "Good. Now when can I tell my friends about the wedding? I was thinking Saturday the fifteenth would be a good choice, don't you? At the reception, we'll serve Big Macs and macadamia nuts."

"Sounds good to me," Joshua said with an indulgent chuckle.

"I couldn't think of anything I'd like more," Bethany added.

"Now about the honeymoon..."

Joshua's gaze didn't leave Bethany as he spoke. "Now, that's one part I plan to take care of myself."

"Anything you say, Dad." Angie looked up at Bethany and winked. "We're going to be so happy."

And they were.

* * * * *

Keepsake

Silhouette Romance ®

COMING NEXT MONTH

#634 HILLBILLY HEART—Stella Bagwell
Morgan Sinclair had been waiting for Lauren Magee to return to
him for years—but he never expected his first love to come back
with such a startling secret....

#635 MAYBE NEXT TIME—Joan Smith
When future congressman Patrick Barron demanded Elinor
Waring return the love letters he'd written, he was up for the
toughest part of his campaign!

#636 PRETTY AS A PICTURE—Patti Standard
Erika Lange was shocked to discover an indiscreet photo of
herself in a magazine—but it all clicked when she met publisher
Richard Marlow....

#637 WOMAN OF THE WEST—Nora Powers
Hope Crenshaw had disguised herself as a man to get a job as a
rodeo clown. Pete Hamilton wasn't fooled—and found himself
enjoying the charade!

#638 SOMEONE TO LOVE—Brenda Trent
When no-nonsense businessman Greg Bradford arrived at Lilly
Neilson's bed-and-breakfast inn, she knew that getting the
handsome workaholic to relax would take some extra effort....

#639 A TRUE MARRIAGE—Lucy Gordon
Gail Lawson had vowed to marry the first man she bumped
into—and a mysterious stranger, Steve Redfern, was more than
happy to block her path....

AVAILABLE THIS MONTH

#628 THE TENDER TYRANT
Victoria Glenn

#629 ALMOST AN ANGEL
Debbie Macomber

#630 RHAPSODY IN BLOOM
Mona van Wieren

**#631 STRANGER AT THE
WEDDING**
Joan Mary Hart

#632 HEART TO HEART
Marie Ferrarella

**#633 A MOST CONVENIENT
MARRIAGE**
Suzanne Carey